ANGELA LYNN CARVER

The Ugly One

Copyright © 2021 by Angela Lynn Carver

All rights reserved. No part of this publication may be reproduced, stored or transmitted in any form or by any means, electronic, mechanical, photocopying, recording, scanning, or otherwise without written permission from the publisher. It is illegal to copy this book, post it to a website, or distribute it by any other means without permission.

This novel is entirely a work of fiction. The names, characters and incidents portrayed in it are the work of the author's imagination. Any resemblance to actual persons, living or dead, events or localities is entirely coincidental.

First edition

This book was professionally typeset on Reedsy.
Find out more at reedsy.com

Contents

	Thank You	v
1	Prologue	1
2	1. Bad Boy Trapped Me	4
3	2. Matchmaker from Hell	9
4	3. Bad Boy Wants Me?	13
5	4. Why Me?	17
6	5. Date My Brother	21
7	6. Date Night	25
8	7. Helping the Bad Boy	29
9	8. Don't Blame Me, I am Innocent!	33
10	9. Trapped with Mr. Bad Boy	37
11	10. Double Date	41
12	11. You are Going Down Good Sir	45
13	12. The First Kiss	49
14	13. Is Someone Jelly?	53
15	14. Stay Out of My Dream	56
16	15. Tug of War	60
17	16. I Don't Want to Dance	64
18	17. Awaiting Punishment	68
19	18. Get Out of My Room!	72
20	19. The Confession	76
21	20. Are You a Vampire?	80
22	21. Pink Haired Nightmare	84
23	22. Parties are Not Fun	88
24	23. This is not a Threesome	91
25	24. I Don't Want This Fantasy	95

26	25. Chasing Virgins	98
27	26. Making a Move	101
28	27. The Birthday Boy	105
29	28. Making Me His	109
30	29. Bringing Back the 80s	112
31	30. Being Kidnapped	115
32	31. Waifu...What?	119
33	32. Jake's Fan Club	122
34	33. Dealing with Insecurities	125
35	34. A New Face	128
36	35. Dinner with Parents	132
37	36. Misunderstanding	135
38	37. Mysterious Occurrence	139
39	38. Interview with a Stalker	143
40	39. Running from the Stalker	147
41	40. Suspect Number Two?	151
42	41. The Confrontation	154
43	Epilogue	158
	Also by Angela Lynn Carver	161

Thank You

Thank you Rosh Calo for designing this amazing cover!

1

Prologue

Hello, my name is Jane and between me and my sister, I am the ugly one. And no, I am not an insecure bitch who likes to complain about my looks all the time.

My sister Liliana is blessed with the beauty genes. She had long flowing blonde hair with bright blue eyes and pink lips that remind you of delicate flower petals.

I, on the other hand, didn't look anything like that. I had coarse brown hair that tangled at the slightest touch, my eyes and lips were also way too big for my face. Okay, maybe I am being too hard on myself. I wasn't completely hideous but when I stand next to her, her beauty overshadowed me and I ended up looking like a troll which is why I tried my hardest not to stand next to her.

I tried to ask my mom if I was adopted, that way I can go look for my birth parents and get away from her but my mom just blew me off.

In high school, I felt insignificant next to her every time guys openly hit on her and pretended like I didn't exist even though I was standing right next to her.

But being extremely beautiful had it's downside too. She had plenty of admirers who were harmless but she also had to deal with a few stalkers and creepy guys hitting on her. At least I was safe from all of that.

"Jane, come on, we are gonna be late!" Liliana said.

It was the first day of school. I was a junior and she was a senior.

"Yay, can't wait to start another year being the understudy of Miss beauty queen," I said.

"Oh, don't start Jane, I told you if you took care of yourself a little better and dressed more...stylish, guys will notice you too!" Liliana chirped.

"I like my sweatpants look, it's much more comfortable," I said.

"Whatever, let's get going," she said and pulled me to the car.

We arrived at school just before the bell rang so I hurried to get to class. My First class had to be located all the way to the end of the building so I decided to make a run for it.

I crashed into something hard and tumbled forward, taking down whoever it was I bumped into. Pretty soon I was staring at a pair of dark brown eyes as I hovered over none other than Jake Morris.

Ah Jake, the high school bad boy. Also, one of many admirers of Liliana. Jake had been trying to get into her pants since ninth grade but Liliana paid no attention to him. She didn't like his *kind* is what she said to me. But that didn't mean he quit trying.

Jake wasn't one of those bad boys you learn about in romance novels. You know the ones that are rough on the outside but secretly a softy on the inside?

PROLOGUE

Nope, not him. He was the actual devil. I secretly call him Damien, the evil child from the movie The Omen. Because he looks like an angel from the outside but in reality, he is most likely a spawn of the devil. I bet if I parted his hair, I'll see the birthmark 666 on his scalp. Okay, I might be exaggerating a little bit but he is the worst. I'll tell you how bad later.

But for now, I have to figure out how to get out of this situation.

2

1. Bad Boy Trapped Me

"Get the fuck off of me," Jake barked.

"Oh ss...sorry Jake," I stammered and got up.

"What are you trying to do? Crush me to death?" he stayed and straightened his shirt.

"I'm trying not to be late to class, so bye!" I waved and tried to leave but he grabbed my arm.

"Not so fast. Aren't you Liliana Brown's sister?" he asked.

"Yeah, so?" I asked. Yes, Jake, we met like ten thousand times before. But go ahead and act like you had no idea who I was.

"So...I need you to do me a favor," he said and smirked.

"Can this wait? I'm already late," I said desperately.

"Fine, you can go. Meet me out back after school, by the fence?" he said.

1. BAD BOY TRAPPED ME

"Sure, bye bye now!" I ran off and sighed in relief to finally get out of his grasp. He scares me.

After school, I debated whether I should go see him or not. What could he possibly want from me?

I decided to go. I stood by the fence and waited.

"Hey," I turned around as I heard his voice.

"Well, I'm here, now what?" I let a nervous laugh.

"You know I've been in love with Liliana for two years right?" he asked.

"More or less," I said.

"Well I've been trying to get her to go out with me but she just acts like I don't exist," his eyes turned dark.

Welcome to my world buddy, I thought.

"Well she is not into the bad boy type," I said.

"That's too bad because she is going to be mine," he insisted.

"Whatever you say," I scoffed. "What do you want me to do about it?" I asked.

"Help me convince her. Maybe you can tell me more about her so I know how to impress her?" he suggested.

"Not a chance buddy. Forget it," I said and tried to leave but he grabbed me and pushed me against the fence.

"I don't think so. You are going to help me whether you want to or not," he demanded.

"Jesus! What is wrong with you? She is not interested, you are not her type, don't you get that?" I yelled.

"Listen...whatever your name is! If you don't help me I'll make sure to make your life miserable in this school. So go homes and think very carefully before rejecting me, got it?" he said.

His dark eyes bored into my eyes. I felt a chill. This guy wasn't joking around and is possibly dangerous. Maybe I can convince Liliana to go on one date at least.

"Okay fine, just let me go. I'll see what I can do. And my name is Jane, you prick!" I frowned.

He let go of me and exhaled.

"Sorry I lost my cool. It's hard for me to control my anger sometimes," he sighed.

Jake? Apologizing? The world must be coming to an end.

"Well you should try harder," I said and ran off.

I don't know how I'm supposed to convince Liliana to date this jerk. It's not like we are super close. I honestly don't even like her. She had always been preoccupied with her own world to pay any real attention to me. As a big sister, she was supposed to protect me, be my friend, but all she did was ignore me. Not once did she try to help me with my insecurities. Maybe Jake and her deserve each other.

1. BAD BOY TRAPPED ME

I knocked on Liliana's door later that night.

"Come in," she yelled.

"Hey Lili, can I talk to you for a second?" I asked.

"What's up Jane?" she asked.

"Well…um…I was just wondering, what do you think about Jake Morris?"

"Who?" she asked.

"You know who, Jake! Tall, muscular, dark brown eyes, kind of scary?" I described him.

"What do I think of him? He is the biggest bully on the planet and his bad-boy act is infuriating," she declared. "Why are you asking about him?"

"Well….he told me he really really likes you and would like to go out with you," I said.

She squinted her eyes at me. "Since when are you friends with Jake Morris?"

"I am not! I just want to help my fellow classmate," I offered.

"Jake is a senior, you are a junior. He is not in your classes. What is going on Jane?" she inquired.

"Okay fine, I'll tell you. He threatened me okay! He said I have to convince you or else…"

"Or else what?" she asked.

"I don't know! And I don't want to find out. So please, just go out with the guy," I pleaded.

"What? No way!" she said.

"Come on Lily, please do this for me! What if he actually hurt me?" I said.

"Forget it, I'm not giving in. He is totally not my type and I'm not going out with some loser just because you are scared of him. Now get out of my room," she said and pushed me out of the room.

Ugh…why does she have to be such a bitch to me? My life was hard enough as it is but now I have to deal with Jake because of her.

I can never count on her, not even once. But I knew Jake wasn't going to let me off the hook that easily.

I remembered in seventh grade, Jake asked Matt Miller to do his homework. Normally Matt did what he was told since Jake beat him up if he didn't. But the day before, poor Matt came down with flu and didn't show up at school with Jake's homework.

Do you think Jake accepted that excuse? Hell no. He waited until the right opportunity for revenge.

There was an annual science project and Matt was looking forward to it. His project was well thought and detailed. On the day before the project was due, Jake sneaked into the classroom and stole it, then burned it on the baseball field. All of Matt's hard work was gone in seconds. Then the next day, he left a note on Matt's locker to let him know whose handiwork it was.

The whole school knew about it but Jake got away with a measly 2 days of detention. It was as if the principal had no desire to defend the bullied. God, I really hated him since then.

That was just one of many horrible things he did to people. Now I have to help him? I'd rather drown him in a tub of holy water.

3

2. Matchmaker from Hell

I wasn't looking forward to school the next day. I kept looking around to make sure I didn't run into Jake. Stupid Liliana and her selfishness.

During lunch, I sat outside to eat my sandwich. He mostly sits inside with his friends and terrorized the unsuspecting nerds so maybe I am safe outdoors.

"There you are, Jane Brown." My heart stopped when I heard Jake's deep voice. Fuck me...

"Oh, hi Jake, I said.

"Well? What did you find out?" he asked casually.

"Liliana's favorite food is chicken fingers?" I said.

"About me, what did you find out when you asked her about me?" he asked, already annoyed at me.

"Oh...um...she said you aren't her type. Sorry Jake," I said.

His eyes glowed with anger again and I felt a familiar chill. I was so screwed.

"Not good enough," he said. "You need to try harder to convince her."

"But Jake... " I whimpered.

"No buts, just fucking do it. There's gonna be a party at my house tonight. Normally I don't invite losers but I'll make one exception for her. I expect you to be there with her," he said.

A party? I was never invited to a party before so I felt kind of excited. I scolded myself in my head immediately. It's not like he was actually inviting me. It was because of Liliana.

"O..okay, I'll try to convince her," I said nervously.

"You better, or else..." he said and walked away.

This was my last chance to convince her so I went to find Liliana.

"A party?" Liliana asked. "Whose party?

"Amanda's," I lied. If I told her it was Jake's house she'd deny me right away. "There will be a bunch of people there so it should be fun right?" I said.

"I guess...since when do you get invited to parties?" she asked.

"Ah...I don't know? I'm a junior now so maybe that's why?" I offered. "Does it matter why? The point is it'll be awesome!" I tried to sound enthusiastic so she'd take the bait.

"Sure, why not. I'll go," she said.

Yes! I'm saved! Maybe she'll change her mind about Jake at the party. I doubted that but at least she is going. I am willing to do anything to save my ass at the moment.

On the night of the party, I mentally prepared myself to face Jake and all the other people from school who act like I don't exist.

Liliana put on a cute romper and curled her hair into loose waves. She looked like a goddess as always. I wish I could look this good in rompers but my butt looks like a pancake when I wear them and let's face it, those outfits make it ten times harder to pee. I am all about comfort and convenience.

So I just put my hair up in a messy bun because I had no idea what to do with it and put on some jeans and a shirt that looked somewhat decent. It's not like I can look cute when she was next to me anyway. Besides, I wasn't hoping to meet anyone. I was trying to ensure my survival.

Liliana agreed to drive so I hopped next to her on the passenger side and we were off to the party!

I looked around for Jake once we arrived at the party. Come on Jake, come over here and sweep her off of her feet and leave me the fuck alone, I thought.

"Who are you looking for?" Liliana asked.

"No one," I giggled nervously. Liliana looked at me suspiciously. I wish I was a better liar.

I suddenly saw Jake. He was wearing a white shirt paired with a leather

2. MATCHMAKER FROM HELL

jacket and jeans. I hate to admit but he looked damn good in that outfit. If he wasn't the biggest jerk of the century, I would've had a crush on him. Looks-wise he was just my type with his longish dark brown hair, deep brown eyes, and a sharp jaw. He was nicely built, probably because he had enough exercise beating up people at our school. I saw him looking at us then he started to walk toward us.

"Hey Liliana, I'm glad you came," he smirked.

"Hey," she said and fidgeted. A scowl already formed on her face like she was disgusted by him. She looked at me with fire in her eyes when she figured out what I had done.

"I'm just gonna go somewhere....else," I said awkwardly and left them alone. I can already imagine how it's gonna go. Not good.

I walked past a few people from my school but they just ignored me as usual. I decided to indulge myself with some underage drinking. I'm at a party, aren't I?

I filled the cup up to the brim and turned around. Perhaps a little too rapidly as I bumped right into a boy's chest and poured my entire beer on his shirt. Some of it splashed on my shirt.

Great, just fucking great. I didn't look at his face right away as I was shell-shocked. With my luck, it's probably Jake again.

I looked up and almost laughed. I must be cursed or something.

It wasn't Jake but someone much worse. It was Aaron, Jake's older brother. He recently graduated from our school but not before he made his mark by being the baddest of the bad.

He had gotten into endless fights and openly smoked on school property. He didn't give two shits about anything. His brother Jake was just a tamer version of him and looked up to him. Most likely learned his evilness from Aaron. In other words, I've really screwed myself this time.

"Don't you look where you move idiot?" he barked and glared at me.

"Oh, shit...I'm sooo sorry!" I cried and tried to blot his jacket with some paper towels.

He stared at me intently. What was he looking at?

Please don't hurt me, I thought to myself.

Am I going to die tonight? How do I keep getting myself into these types of situations? Why god, why?

"Come with me," he said and grabbed my arm. He started to drag me away from where everyone was gathered around.

Oh great, he is taking me somewhere quiet to murder me.

4

3. Bad Boy Wants Me?

"A.. Aaron, where are you taking me?" I asked. I was starting to panic.

"You are gonna help me clean this shit up," he said.

He dragged me inside a room, which I guessed was his room.

"Don't move," he commanded.

I looked at the door helplessly. Should I make a run for it?

He took his shirt off. I've only heard rumors about Morris brothers' hot bodies but now I was finally seeing it in person. As I stared at the hard chest and abs muscles I realized the rumors were all true. But instead of getting excited I was terrified. What was he planning to do here?

"Take your shirt off," he grinned.

"Wha...what?" No way, am I gonna get raped over a spilled beer? I started to panic again.

He threw a plaid shirt at me. "You spilled beer on yours. Put this one on instead.

Oh, he was just trying to help. Why did he have to act like that though? He must be nuts.

"Um...cou...could you turn around?" I said nervously.

"Oh yeah, sorry. Go to the bathroom and change," he said and pointed at his bathroom.

I quickly went inside and shut the door. My heart was pounding. Why am I so scared right now? Since he was always two classes ahead of me I didn't get to see him often. I just heard rumors. Both of the Morris brothers were notorious in our school. Aaron graduated last year so maybe he is not as bad anymore.

I put on the shirt which was way too big but at least it was dry and clean. I got out of the bathroom. Aaron was half lying on the bed and staring at the ceiling. He looked at me as he heard me coming out of the bathroom.

"Thanks for the shirt, I'll go now," I said and started to head for the door.

"Wait!"

I halted.

"Stay for a minute. The party is kinda boring," he said.

True. It was kind of lame. Spilling beer on the former high school bad boy was the most interesting thing that happened so far. I sat down on the chair in front of him.

"You are one of the Brown sisters aren't you?" he asked.

"Yeah! I'm the ugly one!" I blurted out.

He looked startled. "You are what?"

"The ugly one. You know....because Liliana is so pretty?" I explained.

"I guess? Who said you were ugly?" he asked. His gaze was so intense I thought I'd melt to the floor.

"It doesn't matter, I was just joking anyway," I laughed nervously.

He got up and took my hand. Before I could say anything he pulled me toward the bed and sat me down next to him.

"How come I never seen you around here?" he asked.

"I don't go to parties. Besides, you are two classes ahead of me so..."

"Then why are you here?" he asked.

"Well what happened was, I bumped into your brother Jake and he told me to convince my sister Liliana to go out with him or else. So now we are here," I gave him the whole spiel.

"He wants your sister? Why? She is boring as fuck," Aaron said dismissively.

Huh? He doesn't think Liliana is the fruit of a goddess? Well, that's new.

"I don't know? Because she is like the most beautiful girl in school? I wish I can relate but that's not the case. I just got wrapped up in this matchmaking situation by force. Can I please go now?" I said desperately.

3. BAD BOY WANTS ME?

"I guess she is kind of pretty but you..." he stared at me intently again. His green eyes were twinkling.

"What about me? I don't look anything like her I know. I already heard how plain I am from plenty of people so you can just save it okay?" I said and tried to get up but he pulled me back down.

"You aren't plain. You look much more interesting than any girl I've ever met. How about I take you out sometimes and we get to know each other?" he smirked.

What? He was asking me out? Did I accidentally walk inside the twilight zone or what.

I stared at him in shock for a moment. It must be one of his cruel pranks to ask the ugly girl out then break her heart. I am not falling for that. No siree bob.

"Ah...no thanks, I gotta go," I got up and made a run for the door. I need to find Liliana quickly and get out of here.

Before I could find her and make my escape someone grabbed my hand. Aaron?

Nope, it was Jake. Why can't I escape the Morris brothers tonight?

"You!" Jake barked. "You said you would make Liliana love me but she just insulted me and left!" he said.

"I never said I would make her love you. You can't make people love you silly," I let out a nervous laugh.

"I'll make you pay for this, you must've sabotaged this on purpose. You are jealous of her because I'm paying attention to her instead of a plain Jane like you," Jake threatened me.

What the fuck is wrong with this guy? He must be crazy. "How arrogant are you? I'm not even slightly interested in you Jake, let go!" I screamed.

"You aren't going anywhere until we settle this," Jake sneered at me.

"Let the girl go, Jake," someone spoke and I looked up.

Aaron was staring at us with fire in his eyes. If looks could kill, Jake would disintegrate into ashes right now. I was relieved since Aaron was being nice to me and most likely will rescue me from this ruthless boy.

"This is between me and plain Jane, bro," Jake gritted his teeth. Shoot, I knew I was plain but hearing from Jake's mouth was the confirmation I didn't need. Hurtful bastard.

"Let her go or I'll send you to the hospital," Aaron glared at him.

He let go of me. I guess he was scared of his older brother. Thank almighty.

"We are not done, Janey!" Jake said gruffly.

Aaron took my hand and took me outside. "I'll take you home," he said. I nodded. Liliana left with the car so I had no other choice. That bitch.

"So can I take you out or the answer is still no?" he asked when we arrived at the house. Is he for real with this?

"Can I think about it?" I asked, suddenly feeling shy. I've never been asked out by anyone before. Even if it was a prank, it was kind of nice that he noticed me.

"Okay," he said and smiled at me for the first time. He looks ten times more friendly when he smiles. Not to mention gorgeous.

"Tha...thank you for your help," I said and impulsively hugged him. Something stirred inside me when I felt his warmth. I quickly let him go and ran back inside. I really need to be extra careful around the Morris brothers.

5

4. Why Me?

The next morning, the doorbell rang and there were some roses at the doorstep. Must be another one of Liliana's admirers.

I took them inside and set them down on the table. I didn't bother to check the card because who else would it be for?

"Liliana! You got some flowers again!" I yelled.

She ran downstairs excitedly. Her face twisted into a frown when she read the note.

"It's for you," she said and handed me the card.

"Huh?" I was confused.

"These are for you Jane, just read the note," she said, annoyed.

To Jane,

You are beautiful. Don't let anyone tell you otherwise. Please go out with me.

Love

Aaron

I didn't know how to feel the first few minutes. Is he making fun of me? Whatever it was, it's nice to be complimented for once. And these roses are beautiful.

"Who is Aaron? I thought you didn't have a boyfriend?" Liliana asked. I knew this came as a shock to her that I, of all people, is getting flowers from a guy.

"Aaron Morris," I said.

Her face turned dark then she looked downright angry. What was her deal?

"You mean, THE Aaron Morris? Jake's brother Aaron Morris?" she asked again.

"Yes, him. Why do you look like that?" I asked.

"This can't be right," she snatched the card out of hand and read it again. "Why would Aaron Morris ask you out?"

"Why not? Why do you care?" I was curious about her reaction now.

"I've had a crush on him since ninth grade!" she squealed.

"Whaaat! No shit," I laughed out loud. "I thought you said you weren't into bad boy jerks?"

"Aaron is not a bad boy jerk. He was just misunderstood. And he clearly changed after graduation," she said and pointed at the flowers.

"I suppose," I said.

"You can't go out with him!" she cried.

Excuse me? She can't tell me what to do! Who does she think she is?

"I am sorry Lili, but Aaron clearly prefers me over you. Just deal with it," I smirked. Even though I have no desire to go out with Aaron, I could still mess with Liliana.

"Maybe it's a prank. He is just playing you. Or maybe he meant to send these flowers to me and got out names mixed up," Liliana insisted.

Wow, I can't believe how self-centered she is.

"I don't think so," I said nonchalantly. "Besides, his brother likes you. Why don't you go out with Jake instead? He is just as good looking. They almost look alike and he already likes you so all you have to do is say yes to him," I offered.

"No way! Jake is just a pure jerk and so immature," Liliana said.

"Oh, you don't know that! Maybe he is just misunderstood," I said mockingly. I was starting to get tired of this argument.

"Just do this for me and reject Aaron," Liliana said.

Bitch please....after the way she treated me, I am going to date the fuck out of Aaron just to spite her. Just watch me. Whether it is a prank or not, this was my chance to get back at Liliana.

"Well, too bad. Looks like I'll be going out with Aaron after all," I said and

4. WHY ME?

left the room.

Jake cornered me at school the next day. What else is new?

"I told you I wasn't done with you Janey," he said. His dark eyes bored into my soul.

"It's Jane," I corrected him.

"Whatever, I need to ask you, what the hell was that about at the party?" he asked.

"What do you mean?" I asked innocently.

"With my brother! Since when did you two become buddies? Are you fucking him?" he cried.

"Eww, gross. No," I made a face. "I am still as pure as the driven snow, thank you very much," I declared.

"Huh?" Jake looked at me questioningly.

"VIRGIN! I am a virgin," I blurted out without thinking. My face turned red as I embarrassed myself. Why did I tell him that?

"Oh," he said and went quiet. "Then why was he making googly eyes at you?" he asked.

"Fuck if I know, Jakey boy. I've never even talked to him before the party. It's my life goal to avoid the Morris brothers at all costs, which you are totally ruining for me right now," I replied.

"Well, stay away from him. The last thing I need is some loser hanging around my house," Jake said.

"Not a problem. Is that all?" I asked.

"Yes. Why did Liliana treat me like I am a cockroach?" he sounded almost desperate.

"Why don't you ask her? You do realize we go to the same school, right? Go harass her instead," I said. I looked around to see if an administrator was walking by somewhere so I can escape this situation.

"I don't know...I don't want to scare her," Jake said.

But scaring me is okay? What a piece of cow excrement!

"There's literally nothing I can do, Jake. She does not like you. In fact, she told me yesterday that she has a huuuge crush on your brother. So I guess there's that. None of us get to win. Now if you will excuse me, I am going to go and mourn my heartbreak over her stealing my future husband. Bye now," I said quickly and tried to leave but Jake caught my arm again.

"What the fuck did you just say! She likes Aaron!?" Jake shouted so loud that his voice echoed through the walls. Some students looked at our direction in confusion but kept walking past us.

"Calm down, jeez. No need to yell at me. I have no control over this, K?" I exclaimed.

Jake looked like he was deep in thoughts. "This is not good. This is all wrong. She can't like Aaron. She belongs to ME!" he said.

"I know right! Totally. Now can I go, please? I am going to be late for class," I said. I don't know why he is still holding me hostage. He should go interrogate his brother for being better looking and stealing his future wife.

Jake didn't release me and just stared at me intently. I could tell he was cooking up some other plan in his evil little brain. I hoped it didn't involve me in any way.

"I know how you can help me, Janey," he said and smirked.

"H..help you?" I asked. What was he planning?

"I changed my mind about you dating my brother. You are going to date him and keep him away from Liliana so she will forget about him and date me instead," he declared.

Jake you stupid shithead, that's not how life works!

5. Date My Brother

"NO WAY! I am not dating Aaron the former bad boy because you told me to. Forget about it. So far I've been listening to your stupid ideas but this is where I draw the line," I said. I was suddenly feeling courageous.

"You are going to do what I say Jane or I will make your life living hell," Jake said with gritted teeth.

"That's not fair!" I exclaimed. "I hardly know him. Why are you dragging me into your business? It's not like we are friends!" I cried.

"We don't need to be friends. You are her sister so you got all the inside information on her. So now you get to be my wingman," he smirked. "Also the tool to drive away my competition, aka my brother," he added.

Lucky me, I thought. "You are an idiot," I mumbled.

"What did you call me?" he said, anger flashing in his eyes.

"Nothing! I said nothing!" I said quickly.

He didn't press me any farther. "I'll be watching you. I better see you going out on a date with Aaron this weekend," he said and walked away.

I just stood there dumbfounded. What the hell is happening to me? Maybe I was overreacting. Maybe going out with Aaron would be a good thing. Even though I wasn't doing it out of my own free will, this could still turn out to be a great date. Maybe Aaron is an amazing guy and we'll become a couple then one day we'll get married and produce more bad boys and pollute the society.

Gross, what the hell am I thinking? I am losing my mind.

But either way, I could use Aaron as a shield against Jake. If he likes me he will protect me from him, right?

I made up my mind. I will text Aaron and set up a date with him. If nothing else, it'll at least satisfy Jake for now.

I send Aaron a quick text later on. My phone buzzed within 15 minutes indicating I received his reply.

Glad you finally texted me. Did you like the flowers I sent you :)? his text said.

Yes, they are nice, I replied.

Does that mean you changed your mind about going out with me? he asked.

Maybe ;), I replied.

Great, how about a movie and dinner on Friday? he texted.

I thought about it. It wasn't like I had boys lined up to ask me out on dates so my Friday was completely free.

Friday sounds fine, I said.

Perfect, I'll pick you up at 8, he texted back.

Whether it was for the fact that I was a complete loser and had no life, I found myself looking forward to our date. My first date with a boy. A hot guy no less. I shouldn't feel forced and enjoy it. Screw Jake and Liliana, this is my time to shine. It'll be like killing three birds in one stone. I get to go out Friday night, make Liliana jealous, and get Jake off of my back. Maybe I'll ask Aaron to threaten Jake so he doesn't bully me anymore. This could turn out to be the best thing that had ever happen to me.

I was sitting outside of the cafeteria the next day, minding my own business, and eating my sandwich peacefully when Liliana decided to come at me like a bulldozer.

"Jane, you stupid whore!" Liliana screamed at me.

"That's not a very nice thing to call your little sister, Lili. You must be hangry. Here, have a bite of my sandwich and calm your tits," I said and offered her my sandwich.

"Screw your sandwich!" she said and slapped the sandwich off of my hand.

5. DATE MY BROTHER

"Hey!" I screamed and looked down. Does the 5 seconds rule apply for a whole sandwich? Can I still save it? I decided against trying and glared at her. "What'd you do that for?" I asked.

"Why did Jake just tell me that you and Aaron are going out now? I specifically told you not to!" she whined.

"First of all, we are going on our first date on Friday so we aren't officially dating yet, and second, it's none of your business," I said nonchalantly.

"I hate you, you ugly bitch!" Liliana cried.

"Thanks, you aren't exactly the model sister yourself. Bye Felicia," I said and waved my hands.

She stormed off.

"YOU OWE ME A SANDWICH!" I called after her but she was already gone. I don't know what I did to deserve a sister like her.

Well, now I'll have to go hungry all day. I saw Jake standing by his locker flirting with Mandy Smith. So much for being in love with Liliana. What an insolent fuckboy. He looked at me and our eyes met. I looked away quickly and proceeded to open my locker to get my textbooks out. As soon as I closed the door, I almost had a heart attack as Jake was standing right there only a few inches away from my face. Personal space, please!

"Hey Janey," he smirked.

"Look, I said I'll go out with Aaron okay? So stop crowding me," I said.

"I know, thanks. You are going to be great," he said and patted me on the head.

"Good then, we are cool. So why are you here?" I asked.

"I heard you are a math geek," he said casually.

"I am good at math, that is true," I said and looked at him quizzically. I am hardly a geek, Jerk.

"Great, here is my math homework, get it done by Monday," Jake said and shoved a paper in my locker.

"What the fu....no way! I am not doing any more favor for you, asshole," I said angrily. This is getting out of hand now. "Besides, you are a senior and I am a junior which means you have the advanced math class. How would I possibly know how to do this?"

"Because you are smart, Janey. Don't think I don't know you were in the math club last year and won an award in a math competition. That means you can figure this shit out," he sneered.

Huh? How did he know that? I never talked to Jake before.

"Regardless of whether I can do this or not, I am still not doing it! So, take this back and go away jerk!" I said and tried to shove the paper in his jacket. He grabbed my hand and stared at me intently.

"Listen here geek, I am already annoyed that you are not trying hard enough to help me get Liliana. Don't piss me off," he said.

Okay, I've been trying to act tough and stand up to him but he is very intimidating. "Look, Jake. I don't condone cheating. So, how about I help you with it on Friday? Your brother and I are going on a date anyway so I can come over after and do it together?" I asked hopefully. I didn't want to spend any extra time with Jake but I didn't want to be his slave who does his work for him either.

He looked like he was deep in thought as if to consider my offer.

"Alright, I'll let you *help* me, but you are doing most of the work," he declared.

I sighed.

7

6. Date Night

Friday night came and my heart thumped against my chest. I didn't know what to expect but I knew I couldn't let my guard down. It was Aaron Morris after all. I don't remember him much from high school. He was older and unapproachable. Not to mention from a completely different social circle.

I remembered seeing him on rallies and hallways sometimes. He was always surrounded by girls. What's with girls always flocking around the bad boy types? What's so great about being treated like shit? I'll never understand.

I decided to dress up a little. I dug out a summer dress I never wore and put it on. It was a white sleeveless short summer dress with blue flowers on the skirt. Very girly. I straightened my hair with a hot iron so it didn't look coarse and crazy. It took me an hour to get it done. This is why I don't dress up.

I looked in the mirror and felt a little more confident about our *date*. Liliana was right. I don't look half bad when I dress up.

I heard a car outside. It was almost 8 pm so Aaron must be here.

"Could you get the door?" I shouted from my room. My parents weren't home and I wanted Liliana to open the door so she knows Aaron Morris is taking ME out. Suck on that, bitch!

I went outside and saw Lilian still out there talking to Aaron. Must be trying to charm her way into his heart.

"There you are, Jane Brown!" Aaron said, his eyes lit up as he saw me.

"Hi," I said shyly.

"You look great," he smirked.

I blushed. I may have been acting like I was too good for Aaron Morris in my head, but in reality, I was not immune to his boyish good looks and rock hard abs. I'm a teenage girl for gosh sakes.

"Well it was nice talking to you and all but we don't want to be late for our movie. Let's go, Jane," Aaron said to Liliana and took my hand.

"Yes, bye Liliana," I batted my eyelashes at her to piss her off. "Don't wait up," I ended my goodbye with a dramatic hair flip then hopped in the passenger seat. Hope she dies out of jealousy.

"So, where are we going to see the movie?" I asked Aaron.

"You'll see," he smirked.

I took a closer look at him. He was wearing a flannel shirt with some jeans. Nothing too flashy, yet, he looked amazing. Perks of being good looking I guess.

We drove for a while. After 30imutes or so, we finally arrived at our destination. I stared at the big red sign that said, Drive-In Theater.

Ah...the classic. But if he tries to force himself on me like in those old 80s movies, I'm going to kick him in his family jewels.

But he didn't try anything funny. I occasionally caught him stealing glances at me, which was kind of cute. But I couldn't let my guard down completely yet. I needed to figure out his true intentions.

"So, why did you ask me out, Aaron?" I asked after the movie was over.

"I told you, I find you interesting. And I think you are pretty too," he said.

"You should really invest in some new glasses," I suggested.

"I'm serious! Stop putting yourself down so much," Aaron said and stared at me intensely to show me he was serious.

"I just...don't understand. You were one of the most popular guys in school. Even with your bad reputation. Girls love you so you can have anyone you want. So excuse me for questioning your motive," I said.

He grabbed my hand and squeezed it. "Maybe I'm trying to become a better person. I didn't like who I was back then so I figured it's time to change. I'm

6. DATE NIGHT

tired of being labeled as a bully and a bad boy. And I feel like you could help me achieve that goal," he smiled.

Maybe he was telling the truth. He wanted to change. I should stop being so suspicious all the time and just enjoy my time with him.

"Look, it's not like I'm asking you to be my girlfriend or anything. I'm just asking you to give me the chance to show that I can be a good guy too," he said.

"That's...fair," I said quietly. In the back of my mind, I was a tiny bit disappointed that he was not planning on asking me to be his girlfriend.

"Thanks for going on a date with me, I had a good time. I guess I should take you home now, huh?" he asked.

I wish my night ended with this amazing date with him but now it's time for me to face the event I've been dreading all day. Tutoring his douche bag brother.

"No...actually...I was wondering if you can take me to your house instead," I said awkwardly.

Aaron looked at me in shock for a moment. "Whoa, Jane. I didn't realize you were this forward. It's only our first date but if you really want to...."

"WHAT! Oh my God, nooo! It's not what you think," I protested quickly.

"Then why do you want to go back to my house?" Aaron asked. He looked almost disappointed.

"Um...I promised Jake I'd tutor him in Math," I told him. It was a half-truth at least.

Aaron looked at me intently like he was trying to read what was on my mind.

"Why would you want to do that? I thought you guys hated each other. Didn't he bully you? Is this something he is forcing you to do again?" he asked. "Because if he is, you tell me and I'll take care of it."

I thought about it for a second. It was kind of tempting for me to get Aaron to teach Jake a lesson but I didn't want to cause any trouble tonight.

"No, it's not like that. I'm very good at math so he asked for help," I said instead.

Aaron raised his eyebrows but then nodded. "Well, in that case, let's go to my place," he said and started to drive.

I hope Jake doesn't ruin my night, I thought as Aaron pulled into his driveway.

8

7. Helping the Bad Boy

We walked into the house and I instantly regretted coming here. It was quiet now as there was no party going on this time. The house seemed much larger than I remembered.

"Where are your parents?" I asked and looked around nervously.

"They are out of town on a business trip. They are hardly ever home so it's always just the two of us," Aaron said grimly.

So that's why Jake was able to throw those wild parties. They had no adult supervision.

A sudden realization hit me and made me more nervous. I'm about to be home alone with two teenage boys. Ones with a bad reputation, not to mention I was completely defenseless. What the hell was I thinking? I can be so stupid sometimes.

"Oh don't look so scared. We don't bite," Aaron smirked.

"Scared? Who's scared? Not me...haha..." I stammered. "Um, where's Jake?" I needed to get this over with so I can get the hell out of here.

"JAKE!" Aaron yelled, almost busting my eardrums.

No answer.

Maybe I got lucky and Jake forgot about the whole math thing and left the house. I am saved!

"Well, it looks like he is not here. Oh well. I'm gonna call myself an uber and go home. Peace out," I said and proceeded to leave.

Someone grabbed my wrist all of a sudden and pulled me back before I made it to the door.

"Not so fast Janey, you are mine for the next hour," Jake was standing there holding my hand. Fuck...almost made it out the door.

"Let's go study in my room," Jake said and started to pull me away.

"Oh okay, le...let's," I said and looked at Aaron helplessly.

I tried to communicate with him through my eyes and gave him the 'help me' look, but alas, Aaron just stood there and looked at me. His eyes moved from my face to Jake's hand that was tightly gripping my arm. His eyes were dark and I saw a flicker of something in them. Jealousy?

"If you do something to Jane, I swear to god...." Aaron started to say but Jake interrupted him.

"Oh, relax big bro. I'm not going to do anything to your precious date. We are just going to study together like good little pals, right Janey?" he smirked and put his arm around my shoulders.

"Y...yeah. I am a math geek so I'm going to help Jakey here," I nodded my head and chuckled awkwardly.

"Okay, call me if there's a problem," Aaron glared at Jake one last time then left the room.

Jake dragged me in his room. Pretty soon I was trapped inside the room with the biggest jerk in my highschool. Alone.

"Stop looking like a petrified rabbit. I'm not going to hurt you," Jake said irritably.

"Should I be in your room like this?" I asked and fidgeted uncomfortably.

"Why shouldn't you? I don't see a problem," Jake barked and pointed at the desk for me to sit in.

Something dawned on me. Jake probably doesn't think it's weird for me to be in his room alone because he doesn't think of me as a woman. He looks at me as an ugly, wimpy, and nerdy girl he likes to bully.

I didn't know if I should be relieved or be extremely offended.

"So...you and Aaron don't seem to get along too well," I commented as Jake sat down in front of me.

"Nah we have a pretty close relationship," Jake dismissed my claim.

7. HELPING THE BAD BOY

"Huh? Then why are you two always bickering and glaring at each other?" I gave him a puzzled look.

"I don't know. Probably because Aaron recently decided he needed to change and become a good person for whatever reason. I'm sure it's just a phase," Jake said. He looked annoyed.

"Oh no! Not a *good* person! How horrifying," I said sarcastically.

"Shut up," Jake laughed. He took out a piece of paper and shoved it on my hand.

I looked it over then looked at him questioningly. "These are already done," I said.

"Yeah, so?" he said casually.

"So why am I here?" I asked.

"To see if I did it right, obviously," Jake shrugged.

"Couldn't you have done this at school?" I asked.

"You ask too many questions, Jane Brown," Jake smirked. "What did you do with my brother on your little date?" he asked suddenly.

"Um...nothing? We just went to the drive-in theater and..."

"He stuck his tongue down your throat?" he said before I could finish my sentence.

"Ew! It's our first date!" I protested.

"And then, he finger-banged the shit out of you," he continued relentlessly.

"JAKE!" I cried and threw a book at him but he dodged it, laughing.

"It was my first date, so we didn't do anything. Stop being gross," I said angrily.

"Not even a kiss?" he looked at me curiously.

I fidgeted in my seat. How did our conversation turn to this?

"N...no...I'm saving it for someone who likes me a lot. Like, really likes me," I announced.

"I really like you," Jake said. His voice sounded deep and husky.

"W...what?" I was taken aback.

"I really really like you, let's make out," Jake looked into my eyes. His dark brown eyes were twinkling with mischief.

It took me a second to recover from my initial shock. And when I did, I looked closely at his face and realized he was making fun of me.

He couldn't hold it anymore and burst into laughter.

"Ugh, you jerk! Stop messing with me!" I screamed.

"Hah, you stupid bitch! Did you really think I'd ever kiss you?" he said after he stopped laughing then flicked me on the forehead.

"Ouch! Why do you have to be such a bully and an asshole all the time?" I whined as I rubbed my forehead.

"Because I can," Jake sneered.

"Well, I'm leaving. Goodbye to you, shithead," I glared at him and started to walk out the door.

"Aww did I hurt Janey's feelings?" he mocked behind me. "Nice legs by the way!" he hollered.

I just flipped him off and continued to walk. Aaron was standing outside, leaned against his car.

"I'll drop you off," he said.

"Oh no, I can call an uber." I hesitated.

"You were on a date with me so I'll drop you off and that's final," he insisted so I agreed.

"He didn't try anything with you, did he? Jake can be pretty ruthless sometimes but I used to be just like that in high school so I have no right to say anything to him," Aaron shook his head.

I wondered what changed.

9

8. Don't Blame Me, I am Innocent!

The next day at school, I saw Jake harassing Liliana by her locker, and my heart filled with joy. Ah, he is finally taking the initiative and bugging her directly and not trying to use me as a wing woman. Thank the Lord.

He had her pushed against the locker. He was about 6 foot 2 so he towered over her as he hovered over her face staring into her eyes. His lips twisted into a sickly smirk.

Liliana saw me passing by and mouthed 'help me' but I kept walking. Serves her right for being a bitch to me

Jake followed her eyes and saw me. He released her right away and started to walk toward my direction. The fuck...why.

"Janey wait up!" he yelled but there's no way I'm stopping.

Jake caught up to me in the hallway as I was walking to my class. He ran up behind me and yanked my ponytail. I yelped and almost fell backward but he caught me.

"What the hell is your problem?" I snarled. After seeing him way too many times, inside and outside of the school property, I realized I wasn't as scared of him as I used to be. Now I'm just plain annoyed at him.

"I called you," he said and gripped my arm firmly so I couldn't wiggle out of his grasp.

"You had Liliana trapped inside your arms' cage so why did you release her and grab me?" I snapped.

"I need to talk to you about something," Jake said.

"No, I am not going to help you kidnap Liliana," I said.

"That's not what I was going to ask smartass. I wanted to know if you are going to the spring fling dance?" Jake said.

Oh yeah, spring fling dance was coming up. I never really worried about these types of things. It wasn't like I was never invited to these things but I thought they were kind of lame. It was just an excuse for the pretty girls to show off their popularity.

"I don't know. Why do you ask? Let me guess, you asked Liliana and she denied you and now you want me to get in on your scheme to force her to go with you," I said.

"No. Actually, she agreed to go with me," Jake smirked.

What, I didn't see that coming.

"Oh, really? Congratulations," I said.

"There's only one problem," Jake said

"What's that?" I asked.

"She'd only go if you are going," he replied.

I was confused. "I don't get it. What does it matter if I don't go? It's not like we are super close or anything," I said.

"Fuck if I know. The point is if you decided not to go, you better change your mind because you are going," Jake announced.

"Oh, you get to decide my life choices now too? Are you going to decide which college I should apply for?" I rolled my eyes.

Jake pulled me aside and pushed me against the wall. His fiery eyes were boring into my soul. I'll admit his handsome face was looking quite intimidating.

"You are going and that's final Janey," he said.

"You can't hurt me, Jake. Aaron likes me so he will protect me from your idiocy," I said but I wasn't a hundred percent confident about it.

"You wanna bet?" Jake challenged.

I guess I'll be going to the dance.

8. DON'T BLAME ME, I AM INNOCENT!

A week has passed and the Spring fling dance was approaching quickly. I'll admit I was sort of excited to attend this year. Why? Because this time, I actually had a date.

I had been texting and talking on the phone with Aaron a lot. That's right, the former bad boy and the plain Jane are now friends. I could tell Aaron liked me and wanted to go out with me again so I asked him to the dance. Aaron was pleased and Of course, Jake was pretty happy about it.

But do you think he was overwhelmed with gratitude towards me and ran up to me and enveloped me in a thank you embrace? Not a chance in hell. His bullying against me continued.

Like today, I was strolling down the hallway, humming my favorite tune, then all of a sudden, I felt two hands pushing me and I tumbled forward. I dropped my binder which somehow unbound itself and all of my papers flew across the room.

I looked up, horrified. Jake was standing in front of me, laughing his ass off.

"You son of a biscuit, how could you!" I cried.

"Oh no, Janey! How did you fall on a dry floor? You are so clumsy," Jake cooed.

"Ugh! I know you pushed me. I felt your arms on my back, asshole," I sneered.

"Stop imagining things Janey, I would never touch you intentionally." Jake sneered back at me.

"Stop calling me Janey. My name is Jane, JANE!" I screamed on top of my lungs.

"What's all this commotion? Ms. Brown, why are you sitting on the dirty floor?" one of our administrators, Mr. Green walked up to me and asked.

"Jake pushed me!" I yelled and pointed at Jake who just glared at me.

"Is this true Mr. Morris? Did you push her?" Mr. Green asked him.

"No way. Jane is clumsy and putting the blame on me so she doesn't look like an idiot," Jake said.

"Liar!" I cried.

"Alright, you two. Go to the principal's office. Right now," Mr. Green ordered.

"But....." I started to protest but stopped when he glared at me.

"No arguing. I will not tolerate childish behavior in this school. Mr. Morris, you better help her pick up her papers and head to the office in 10 minutes." he said.

"Yessir," Jake said sarcastically.

Mr. Green shook his head and left. Jake started to pick up the papers with me. "Nice going, Janey. You got us both in trouble," he said.

"ME? It was all your fault, you bully!" I groaned.

"Whatever. Let's just get this over it. Lunch is about to start and I don't want to miss it. I'm hanging out with Liliana today." he said.

I was surprised. Was Liliana warming up to Jake? Does she like him now? I wondered. In that case, why won't he just leave me alone?

We went to the principal's office and sat in front of him. Our principal Mr. Garcia was a stoic, humorless man who didn't take any shits from anyone. I was a little scared.

"This is the third time you are visiting my office, Jake," Mr. Garcia said and gave Jake a disappointed look.

Jake didn't say anything.

"And you Jane, I'm very surprised you are here. You are usually a quiet and brilliant student. How did you get mixed up with Jake?" he asked.

"I didn't! It was all his fault!" I accused Jake.

"Regardless of whose fault it was, I'm going to have to punish you both for creating commotion in the hallway. After school is over, you are to spend two hours cleaning and organizing the basement," Mr. Garcia declared.

"No fucking way!" Jake yelled.

"Watch your language son," Mr. Garcia warned him.

"Why do we have a basement?" I wanted to know.

Mr. Garcia just ignored me and waved his hand dismissively. "Get to it before I lose my patience."

Great. Spending alone time with Jake for two hours is not what I had in mind today.

10

9. Trapped with Mr. Bad Boy

"Nice going Janey," Jake snarled at me.

We met up in the basement after school, much to my dismay.

"This is all your fault, buddy. YOU pushed me!" I protested.

"Whatever," he waved his hands in dismissal. "Let's just get this over with so I can go home," he said gruffly.

"Yeap, let's...why don't you start by moving those boxes over there and I'll sweep the floor," I offered.

Jake didn't argue anymore. He went over to the corner and started to move stuff around. I picked up the broom and started sweeping. Jake sneezed a few times as the room was dusty. His eyes were slowly turning red. Dust allergy?

I guess my sweeping skill was rusty because I was doing a terrible job. All I did was move the dirt around and made the room dustier.

We worked together quietly for the first half-hour. I was surprised he didn't attack me with smart-ass remarks or call me nasty names for this long. Must be a new record for him.

"Would you move your fat ass a little faster? I am sick of this dust already," Jake remarked after a while.

And there it is ladies and gents, Jake is back with his insults. "I am sweeping as fast as I can. Just shut up and do your part," I snarled.

"What exactly am I supposed to be doing anyway?" he asked.

"He wants us to stack those boxes neatly on the side of the room so there will be room for more things here. So, chop-chop. Let's use those muscles and start to lift those boxes since I can't," I said.

"Oh, you noticed?" Jake smirked and flexed his arms. I rolled my eyes.

We worked some more. Thankfully, he was cooperating and not acting like an imbecile for once.

"Phew, all done. Let's get out of here," I said. I was exhausted and couldn't wait to get out of this half-lit, musty basement.

"Thank god," Jake said and got up the stairs ahead of me. What a gentleman, I thought sarcastically.

"Uh oh," he said loudly as he pulled on the door handle.

"What?" I asked. I didn't like the sound of that.

"I think the door is jammed," he said.

"Ha ha, very funny Jakey boy. I am too tired for your dumb prank right now," I said.

"I am not kidding. This is really stuck," Jake said and pulled on the door handle again.

"Get the fuck out of my way," I said and pushed him aside. I turned the doorknob several times and pulled but the door was really stuck. Oh hell no.

"Do you believe me now, Genius?" Jake said sarcastically.

"No way, this can't be happening! I can't be stuck here with you! We need to get out of here!" I cried.

"No shit Sherlock," Jake said and rolled his eyes.

I started to bang on the door. "HELP! IS SOMEONE OUT THERE? WE ARE STUCK!" I yelled. I didn't hear any footsteps approaching. No one was around to come to rescue us as the school was over.

"Jesus, stop yelling. Call someone on your cellphone or something," he suggested.

I took my phone out and stared at it. "Oh my god, I have no signal down here!"

"Are you fucking kidding me?" Jake barked.

"Um...what about your phone?" I asked.

He dug into his pockets for his phone but then made a sour face.

"What is it?" I asked frantically.

9. TRAPPED WITH MR. BAD BOY

"Shit...I forgot. Ms. Levy confiscated my phone in class earlier and forgot to give it back to me. So, I don't have it on me," Jake said awkwardly.

Oh, fuck my life.

"No, no, noooooo!" I screamed and paced back and forth.

"Jesus Christ, what the fuck is wrong with you?" Jake said irritably. "Calm the fuck down, would you?"

"How can I calm down! We are going to be trapped in here for who knows how long! Why aren't you panicking?" I said frantically.

"Because I am not a whiny bitch like you. We aren't going to be trapped in here forever. Someone will know we are missing and come look for us I am sure," Jake said hopefully.

But how long will that take? No one at home cared about me. My parents were always out working late and Liliana probably wouldn't even notice I was gone.

"I can't wait that long. This room is too small...I can't...breathe..." I started to hyperventilate all of a sudden.

I knew Jake was probably thinking I was being dramatic but I was truly having a panic attack. This room was cold and dark. The dust was starting to trigger my asthma. I haven't had an asthma attack since I was little but I could feel it coming back as I was panicking. I laid on the ground on my stomach and started to wheeze.

"Um...Jane? Stop acting crazy," Jake said.

I couldn't pay attention to him as I was too busy dying. His voice sounded far away. I held my chest and tried to calm down but my mind was going blank every second. I felt two arms grabbing me and lifting me up then holding me.

"Hey calm down. Jane? Can you hear me?" Jake was saying. He sounded concerned for once.

"I can't breathe...I can't..." I gasped for breath and started to shake.

"JANEY! For fuck's sake! What do I do?" Jake sounded panicked. I could see him hovering over me but my vision was blurry.

I felt warm all of a sudden. He was hugging me.

"Shhh...just breathe..." he said and unzipped my hoodie to give me some air. Thank god I was wearing a tank top underneath today.

He slipped his hand inside my tank top. I felt goosebumps all over my body as I felt his warm hand on my back. Is he trying to sexually assault me at a time like this?

"W..what are you doing," I stammered and tried to wiggle his hand away but I was too weak.

"Stop moving, I am going to massage your back. It'll help you calm down," he scolded me.

I was going to fight him some more but stopped when he started to caress my back. I automatically put my head on his chest and closed my eyes. His hand felt so calming and warm. I felt my breathing returning to its normal state. My body stopped shaking.

"Is this making you feel better?" his voice sounded sweet and gentle. This wasn't the Jake I was used to. Why couldn't he act like this all the time? I nodded against his chest.

"Well good. You were starting to scare me a little. I thought I'd have to hide your dead body down here," he scoffed.

"You can stop touching me. I am good now," I lifted my head off of his chest.

"Are you sure? Your boobs are kind of nice..."

"JAKE!" I yelled and pushed him off of me and punched him on the chest.

11

10. Double Date

"Ouch! Why did you hit me? Is this how you thank me for helping you?" Jake frowned.

"Well, helping me doesn't involve feeling me up, asshole!" I cried. "But thanks...." I added. He really did help me. I was feeling much calmer and started to breathe normally again. I guess it was all in my head.

"Can't believe you had a panic attack over this. We've only been stuck for like 20 minutes. Such a nerd," Jake shook his head.

I just ignored him and looked at my phone. I only need one bar to send a text so I started to walk around, trying to catch a signal.

"Any luck?" he asked.

"I don't know.....wait...I think I got something!" I said excitedly. I decided to text Aaron. He has a car and he shows that he cares about me sometimes.

Help! I am trapped in the school basement with Satan!

I typed it and hit send. The text came back with a message failed signal. Fuck...

"Wait, Jake. You are taller! Hold the phone high over your head. It helps," I suggested.

He nodded and did what he was told. "Hmm...still not high enough. Come on, get on my shoulder," he said.

"Whaa...no way!" I protested.

"Get your ass over here," Jake's heated eyes bored into my soul.

"I...I'm too heavy, you'll get hurt," I hesitated.

"On what planet?" Jake became impatient and came to me himself. He grabbed my waist and before I could say anything else, he flung my body over his shoulder like I was a big sack of flour.

"Jake, what the fuck! Put me down!" I screamed.

"Just shut up and check your phone again," Jake said irritably then grabbed my hips to lift me up on his shoulder. How much does he work out to get this strong? Sweet Jesus.

I decided to pardon his hands on my ass just this once and concentrated on my phone. I kept hitting the send button and hallelujah! It sent!

"Success! Yasss bitch! We did it!" I screamed. "Now kindly put me down and remove your hands from my ass please," I said to Jake.

He chuckled and put me down. "Thank god. I thought I was about to get suffocated with your big butt," he remarked.

"I don't have a big butt," I protested. "Do I?" I was unsure now.

"Jeez...I'm just teasing. Chill out with that insecurity of yours," Jake said and gave me an intense look. I didn't realize he noticed I was insecure about myself.

We sat there in silence for a few more minutes and all of a sudden I heard someone rattle the doorknob.

"We are down here!" I yelled frantically.

Someone forcefully pushed the door open. Jake and I both jumped up and strode toward the stairs.

Aaron was standing there along with the school janitor. He had a worried expression on his face.

"Aaron! My hero!" I screamed and threw myself on his arms. He laughed and hugged me. "I thought I'd be stuck down here with this demon child forever!" I said, pointing at Jake.

"Yeah, speak for yourself. Like I want to be stuck looking at your hideous face all day," Jake commented.

"Alright you two, let's go home," Aaron rolled his eyes. "Poor Jane, glad you aren't hurt," he said and cupped my cheeks.

"Yeah, I'm fine too. Thanks, bro," Jake said sarcastically.

10. DOUBLE DATE

Aaron just ignored him and drove me home first. I went inside and flopped down on my bed, completely exhausted. This had been a long day. I thought about Jake and how he helped me despite his crude behavior from time to time. Maybe he wasn't as bad as he made himself out to be.

Aaron asked me to hang out with me the next day and I agreed right away. Anything to get away from the house. Besides he was the real hero for saving me from the basement.

"Where are you going tomorrow?" I turned around as I heard Liliana's irritating mousy voice. She must've overheard me talking to Aaron about our date.

"Going out," I said. "We are going to play Laser tag at a place called The Main Event."

"With Aaron?" she asked. I could practically smell the jealousy on her.

"Of course, Darlin. Who else?" I replied dramatically.

"Are you two a thing now?" she asked.

"It's nothing official yet, but who knows what the future holds," I shrugged.

Liliana looked annoyed. "He'll get tired of you eventually, you know. Guys like that don't stay with one person for too long. Especially someone as plain as you," she commented.

"Well Aaron Morris happens to think I am beautiful so I guess you are wrong," I tried to sound confident but deep down I didn't believe it myself. What if Aaron was just hanging out with me because he liked that I was a little different than the other girls? What if eventually, he doesn't think that's not enough anymore and decides to find someone prettier? I was just starting to like him so that would sting.

I decided not to think about it too much and went to sleep.

He pulled up on my driveway the next day, Looking ultra hot in his grey jeans and a white t-shirt. I hate him for being prettier than me.

"Hey Jane," he said and gave me a sexy grin. "Ready for some fun?"

I am ready to rub my hands all over those abs, the thought flew across my mind before I could stop it. What is wrong with me. I was thinking like a horny teenager. Bad Jane!

"Y...yeah," I said nervously. I really need to calm down.

The good news is, I love playing laser tag so I'm pretty sure once I get there, I won't be as nervous anymore.

We finally arrived at the place. I stood by the door and waited while he buys is tickets.

"Oh, em gee Janey! What a coincidence!"

My heart skipped a beat as I heard Jake's deep voice calling out to me. Why oh why. Why can't I escape him?

I slowly turned around to glare at Jake. Oh great, he brought Liliana too. I bet she invited him to come here so she can ruin my alone time with Aaron. I should've never told her where I was going.

"What are you doing here?" I demanded to know.

"To play laser tag obviously," Liliana said.

"You hate laser tag. You said all that running around makes your hair sweat," I said.

"Well Jake loves it so I like it now," Liliana announced.

"Since when do you like Jake?" I countered.

"Ladies, I'm right here," Jake said in an annoyed tone. "The point is, we are all here. Did ya miss me, Janey?" Jake asked and pinched my cheek.

"Get your hands off of her," Aaron said suddenly. He was back from the ticket booth already. "Why are you here?" he asked.

I sighed. I was really looking forward to spending time with Aaron and get to know him more.

12

11. You are Going Down Good Sir

"So Aaron and I are going to be in the team against your team," I said.

"Are you sure you want to do that? Because you are definitely going to lose against Jake Morris, the laser tag champion," Jake declared. "Scared yet?" he smirked.

"You are wrong! You are the one that should be scared, Morris. prepare to feel my wrath!" I cried and started to stretch my legs. The bad boy is going down tonight!

I may be plain, unpopular, and invisible among social circles, but when it comes to video games and laser tag, I was invincible. Jake is in for a treat.

The person in charge of the game divided the players into two teams. I purposely went against Jake's team because I promised him death.

"Are you sure you don't want to play with me instead of against me? I don't want to make you cry," he smirked.

Oh please...

"Pfft...just worry about saving your own buttocks, good sir," I dismissed him.

Jake stared at me with an amused look on his face. He probably expected me to be the shy little Jane I usually am but I turn into a different person when I'm around the things I love.

"Don't worry Jane, I got your back," Aaron had a serious expression on his face.

"Can we just get this thing started? You guys are so dramatic," Liliana rolled her eyes.

Pretty soon the game began and it was time to show him who was the boss. I grabbed Aaron's hand and took cover.

"Here's what we are going to do, I'm going to hide behind the wall, and you are going to flash your abs at Liliana to distract her so I can sneak up on her and MURDER HER!" I declared.

"You are trying to use me as bait," Aaron looked hurt.

"There's no time for a sense of morality. We must not let them win!" I squealed.

Aaron laughed and proceeded to shoot at some other people.

Pretty soon we were down to a few members. Liliana lost a while ago since she didn't like to play anyway. Jake was still alive somewhere. He wasn't joking when he said he was good at this.

"Ugh! He got me!" Aaron screamed then left the room.

It was between me and Jake now. I stayed hidden and looked around. Where was this sneaky bastard?

Then I saw him. I jumped up but just as I was about to shoot him the light turned off and the room became pitch black.

Awe come on! I almost had him.

"Attention customers. We are experiencing a short power outage, please stay where you are."

Someone announced on the intercom.

I took a few steps ahead and suddenly a hand grabbed my wrist, startling me. Someone grabbed my waist and pulled me closer to him.

"Don't move around in the dark, you'll get hurt," Jake whispered. I got goosebumps as I felt his breath on my neck. He was way too close to me.

"Jake, stop breathing on my neck," I whispered.

"Sorry, I can hardly see anything," he whispered back but still held on to me. Warmth spread through my body from his hands on my waist.

"You can let go of me. I'm not going to escape," I chuckled nervously.

The light turned back on all of a sudden and Jake let go of me. Aaron and Liliana walked in to look for us.

11. YOU ARE GOING DOWN GOOD SIR

"Hey, are you guys okay?" Aaron asked.

"We are fine," I said.

"Except, Jane stepped on my toe. I think she broke it," Jake said.

"I did not! Stop spreading lies," I said dismissively.

"Let's get out of here. I'm taking you out to eat," Aaron said.

"Yes! Food, I like it," I declared.

"I'm hungry too," Liliana whined.

"Well, you guys go find your own food. Aaron and I are going somewhere to spend time together. Alone," I announced.

"That's right," Aaron smirked.

"But..." Liliana started to say something more but Jake interrupted.

"Fine by me. Let's go, Liliana," he said and dragged Liliana away. He had a scowl on his face like he was angry about something. Maybe he was hoping to spend alone time with her but she dragged him in here instead.

Aaron and I went to a restaurant near the laser tag place. I was so hungry I felt like I could die.

"Sorry about Jake and Liliana crashing our date but we are finally alone," Aaron grinned. We just finished having dinner and now sitting in his car on the parking lot.

"Yeah, thank God. He wouldn't leave me alone ever since I bumped into him at school," I rolled my eyes.

"Maybe he has a crush on you?" Aaron looked thoughtful.

"Jake? Has a crush on ME? Hahahaha you are so funny Aaron!" I let out an exaggerated laugh at that ridiculous notion.

"It's not that crazy. When we were kids, he decapitated my favorite transformers action figure because he really wanted it and I wouldn't give it to him," Aaron said.

"Oh great, so you are telling me he might decapitate me if he likes me. That's just lovely," I frowned.

Aaron laughed and leaned closer. "Enough about Jake, let's talk about us," he said quietly.

"U...us?" I asked. His intense eyes make me so nervous.

"What do you think about me? Do you like me?" he said and paused for my reaction.

Do I like Aaron? At first, I wasn't sure but he is turning out to be a pretty decent guy. I really think I like him.

"Yes, I like you," I said.

"Good. Then, is it okay if I kiss you? I've been wanting to do it since I met you. I really like you, Jane," he said.

My first kiss. It was finally happening!

I nodded in agreement. Aaron smiled and leaned closer to my lips.

"WAIT!" I yelled. Aaron snapped his head back in confusion.

"I've never kissed anyone before so what if I'm bad at it?" I said.

Aaron laughed. "Just leave it up to me," he said and proceeded to kiss me again so I closed my eyes.

13

12. The First Kiss

He pressed his lips on mine and kissed me softly. It wasn't anything like what they show in the movies or how they described in romance novels. I didn't hear any fireworks go off or my heart didn't jump out of my rib cage and run away. It was short and it was sweet. His lips felt soft and warm and he was a good kisser. I mean, I guess he was. I wouldn't know since I had no one else to compare it too.

He gazed into my eyes with those gorgeous green eyes and I felt like I was going to melt. Why did he have to be so handsome?

"I am glad I got to be your first kiss, Jane Brown," he said and smiled.

"I totally sucked, didn't I?" I asked. I just had to know the truth.

"No, of course not. I love your lips," he said quietly.

"These?" I gasped and pointed at my lips. "You don't think they are way too big for my face? I've always felt awkward about them," I said sadly.

"Are you kidding? They are gorgeous!" Aaron exclaimed. My heart did a little flip. His reaction and comment seemed sincere. Maybe I can finally love this part of my face now.

"Thank you," I whispered. "I am glad you are my first kiss too. You are not at all like how I imagined you to be," I said.

Aaron looked sad all of a sudden. "I am trying to change. I don't like the way I was in high school," he remarked.

"We all make mistakes. What matters now is that you are a better person now," I said reassuringly.

"I want to kiss you again, Jane," Aaron said and looked at my lips with his lusty eyes.

I leaned over and pressed my lips on his. This night was turning out to be amazing.

I almost bit his lips as the Star Trek theme song started to play on my cellphone. Gosh, I really should've changed my ringtone. Aaron must think I am a nerd now.

I quickly picked up the phone and answered it.

"JANE! You need to come pick me up, right now!" Liliana squealed on the other line.

"What? But why? Where is Jake?" I asked.

"That asshole left me on the side of the street! We had an argument and he just told me to get out of the car then he drove off!" Liliana whined.

I couldn't help but giggle at the hilarity of her situation. That's what she gets for being a complete bitch all the time. For once I was grateful to Jake for not putting up with her shit.

"Are you laughing? How can you laugh when I am in this horrible situation?" Liliana cried.

"Okay, okay just calm down. I'll ask Aaron to come get you so take a chill pill," I said.

"Hurry up! There's a creepy homeless guy across the street who is staring at me so I am scared," she said frantically.

Ah...maybe the creepy homeless guy will take her away and make her the queen of his cardboard home. Then finally, I'll become the favorite daughter.

But that was just a pipe dream. I sighed and turned to Aaron and told him about the situation.

"About time you got here. What took you so long?" Liliana said as soon as we arrived.

"Um...excuse me, you are welcome for coming to your rescue," I waved my hands in frustration.

Liliana saw Aaron come up behind me and her entire demeanor changed.

12. THE FIRST KISS

She changed from the evil stepsister mode to the googly-eyed Cinderella mode.

"Aaron! Oh my god, thank you sooo much for coming to get me," Liliana cried and threw herself in his arms.

Smooth bitch, real smooth.

Aaron just stood there awkwardly and tried to recover from her sudden attack. "There, there, we are here now," he said. "What happened?" he asked.

"Your brother, he is a massive jerk!" Liliana replied.

"Facts, but what exactly happened?" he asked again.

"Well, he was going to take me to dinner so I picked the restaurant. He said it was too expensive and offered a cheaper alternative instead. So I told him to stop being stingy and take me to the one I like but he won't budge. I finally agreed to go to his stupid restaurant, but I hated the food there because it was so greasy, you know?" she paused.

Aaron nodded and encourage her to go on.

"I complained about the food, because of course, why wouldn't I? One thing led to another and he got angry at me and called me a bitch so I slapped him. He then told me to get out of the car and drove off. He just left me here all alone in the dark, Aaron!" she sobbed and hugged him again.

Bitch, get off my man, I thought to myself.

I was slightly shocked that Jake ditched her for such a small matter. For someone who claimed to be in love with her, he sure didn't care enough to dish out some money. I was secretly glad he didn't tolerate her gold-digging ways. Good for you, Jakey boy.

"Let's take you girls home," Aaron said and we headed towards his car.

When we finally arrived home, I looked at Aaron and smiled. I wondered if he was getting tired of rescuing people. First me and Jake, now Liliana.

"Thank you for everything, Aaron. You are my hero," Liliana said sweetly.

"Oh don't mention it," he said and turned back to me.

"I had a good time with you, Jane. We should do this again sometimes," he said and moved closer to me.

"Me too. Thank you for taking me out. Maybe next time it'll be just the two of us," I said pointedly. I could feel Liliana fuming in the background.

Aaron didn't say anything and leaned over to kiss me goodbye. I grabbed his neck and deepened the kiss just to piss Liliana off.

I practically danced my way into the house. I was swimming in bliss.

"So, you aren't going to give up on Aaron, are you?" Liliana asked.

"Why would I do such a thing? Aaron is amazing," I said with stars in my eyes.

"How can you do this to me? You can tell how much I like him! How can you do this to your own sister?" she screeched.

Ugh, not this again.

"Just give up already. Aaron is into *me*. You saw how he kissed me," I said.

"Pfft...that looked like you were kissing our cousin," Liliana said.

"Or, you were just jelly," I countered.

"Or, you guys have sexual chemistry of two wooden pillars," she said.

"La la la la I can't hear you, I am too busy planning my next date with Aaron, so bye," I went inside my room and slammed the door shut. She can complain all she wants but she will not stop me from dating Aaron Morris, I promised myself in my head.

14

13. Is Someone Jelly?

I saw Jake hanging out outside of the cafeteria. He was leaned over on a pillar, smoking a cigarette. I had to give him props for his boldness because if an administrator caught him smoking, he would be in serious trouble.

I couldn't help but be curious about how he felt about his 'break up' with Liliana so I approached him.

"Hey," I said quietly.

Jake looked up and smirked. "Hey Janey, you are talking to me first? That's weird," he said.

"First time for everything I guess," I replied.

"What's up?" he asked.

"So...you and Liliana are over, huh?" I asked.

"Yup. She turned out to be too fake for me. I couldn't deal with her bitchy attitude," he shrugged.

You and I both buddy, I thought. "I could've told you that but you'd never listen to me," I said.

"Why are you asking? Does that make you happy that I am not with her anymore?" he raised his eyebrows and moved an inch closer to me.

"Huh? Why would I be happy? I don't care who you are with. But I am glad you'll finally stop harassing me about her," I said.

"Will I now?" His eyes were twinkling with mischief. I didn't like the way he was looking at me.

"Yes, you will. You have no reason to bother me now. I don't have any other beautiful sisters for you. I am shutting down the matchmaking business," I declared.

"Well that's just too bad," he chuckled.

"Well, it was nice chatting with you but I am gonna go," I said and proceeded to leave but he grabbed my hand.

"Stay for a minute. Lunch isn't over for another ten minutes," he said.

"Eh...no thanks. That smell of smoke is killing me. I think I can feel my asthma coming back," I protested.

He dropped the cigarette on the ground and stepped on it. "There, it's gone," he said and stared at me intently.

I blushed a little. He did that for me? That was oddly considerate of him.

"I want you to keep me company," he said quietly.

I shifted my legs uncomfortably. He was acting kind of weird. Almost like a nice guy and it was creeping me out.

"So, what did you and Aaron do after we left? Did you guys have fun?" he asked.

My eyes lit up when I thought about Aaron and the kiss we shared. I guess Jake noticed my change of demeanor because he was staring at me harder now.

"I had a great time. I finally had my first kiss!" I blurted out. I couldn't contain my excitement.

"He kissed you?" Jake asked in almost an accusatory tone.

"Y..yes?" I asked. The atmosphere between us suddenly shifted. Jake's eyes were dark.

"Does that mean, you really like him?" he asked.

"Um..yes, I think so. He is a great guy and we get along great. Besides, he thinks I am pretty," I said.

"Well, he is a fucking idiot," Jake said angrily. What was his deal?

"That's not very nice. Are you calling me ugly?" I pouted.

"That's not what I meant," Jake waved his hand dismissively. "I just think you are moving too fast with him."

13. IS SOMEONE JELLY?

"Anyway, it's none of your business, so..." I said.

Jake glared at me with fire in his eyes. Why was he so angry all of a sudden?

"The bell is about to ring so I am gonna go," I said quickly.

"Then why the fuck are you still standing here? Get out of my face," Jake barked.

I should get used to his meanness but I couldn't help but feel a bit hurt about his coldness toward me. He is such a jerk.

15

14. Stay Out of My Dream

"Mmm....that feels good. Please don't stop," I moaned.

"I don't plan on it," Aaron said and flashed me his sexy grin. He leaned over and kissed me on the neck. "You want me to ravage you, don't you?" he asked and bit my neck.

"Yes please," I said and ready to feel him inside of me.

"I am gonna fuck you so hard, Janey," he growled.

Huh? Since when does Aaron call me Janey?

"You are mine, Janey," he said in a deep and husky voice.

Wait a minute...something doesn't seem right. This voice...it doesn't sound like Aaron.

"Um...Aaron?" I whimpered. The figure on top of me looked up and hovered over my face and I found myself staring at a pair of deep brown eyes.

But Aaron has green eyes, that means...

JAKE!?

"Aaaaaaaaaaaah!" I screamed and jolted awake.

Did I just have a wet dream starring Jake? Fuck no!

"UGH gross!" I yelled.

"Will you shut up? I'm trying to sleep," Liliana shouted from the next room.

I stood up and ran to the kitchen and gulped down some ice-cold water. I tried to shake off Jake's naked body out of my head. This is wrong, this is all wrong. He couldn't even leave me alone in my dreams!

14. STAY OUT OF MY DREAM

The next day, I walked around like a zombie as I felt like poop from sleep deprivation.

I saw Jake flirting with Jenny Patterson and the images from my dream flashed in my mind again.

"Eeek!" I let out a screech and ran the opposite way.

I didn't go too far as someone caught my arm.

"What the hell was that about?" Jake stood in front of me, his eyebrows were raised in concern.

"Um...nothing, I saw a bug," I said quickly.

"Really? It sure looked like you saw me and screamed than skittered away," he looked at me suspiciously. "Did something happen?" he asked.

Yes, Jake, you boned me in my dreams and took my innocence.

"Nothing happened, GOSH!" I said. My face was flushed red, contradicting my claim.

"Janey, what...." he started again but I smacked his hand off of mine.

"It's Jan....ugh, nevermind! Just keep those abs away from me!" I cried and ran off. I couldn't stand being this close to him right now. The memory of the dream was too fresh in my mind and I'm utterly traumatized. I wonder what he thought of my outburst. I hope he didn't suspect anything.

But there was nothing to suspect because it was only a dream. The dream was just confused between the brothers. It was meant to only allow Aaron, not Jake!

I tried to think about anything else other than Jake all day.

At the gym, it was time to run laps. My least favorite activity. I was pretty out of shape so by the time I was on lap number two, I was gasping for breath. So I stopped to take a break. I saw Jake across the field, preparing for a practice football game.

"Alright boys, it's gonna be shirts Vs. Skin!" the coach announced and Jake took his shirt off.

Oh, you've got to be shitting me right now.

I tried to peel my eyes away from Jake's body but my eyes kept wandering back to it.

He was running around with the others with his shirt off. His tanned, muscular body was glistening in the sun.

I'm going flush my eyes with holy water when I get home, I decided. I gulped as he looked back at me and saw me staring. He grinned.

Oh, ma gawd he knows I'm having impure thoughts about him!

No, no, no. Stop it, Jane! Think about Aaron instead. He is so much more handsome and not a complete jerk like Jake.

"I like Aaron, not Jake," I muttered under my breath, as if to convince myself.

"What about me?"

I almost had a mini heart attack when I heard his voice near me.

"What? I didn't say anything about you," I shook my head violently.

"You are acting weirder than usual," Jake said as he towered over me.

"Well I'm a weird person, deal with it," I said.

"True. Anyway, I came here to ask you why you were staring at me?" Jake asked and sat down in front of me.

"You are mistaken. I would never stare at the likes of you!" I declared.

"Oh yeah? I could practically feel your eyes burning a hole through me. Do you like what you see?" he grinned.

"What? Ew no..." I denied.

"Then why are you blushing? You like my muscles, don't you Jane? You wanna touch them?" he said and grabbed my hand and placed it on his chest.

I flinched and tried to take my hand away but he firmly held it in its place. I suddenly felt hot and bothered. Dammit...he does have a hot body.

Think about Aaron, think about Aaron, think about Aaron, I kept repeating in my head.

He released my hand, but I didn't remove it right away. "Alright, I'm gonna stop teasing you now. You got that petrified look on your face again," Jack laughed. "You may take your hand back now," he winked.

"Ah yeah...thanks," I said awkwardly and retreated. "I gotta go," I stood up and hurried off. I could feel his eyes on me the entire time.

What was wrong with me, getting all flustered over a dream? If anything, it was more like a nightmare! Me and Jake don't even get along so there was

14. STAY OUT OF MY DREAM

no way I should lust over him. I should focus on someone who does care. Someone like Aaron.

Fortunately for me, I didn't run into Jake again after that.

I suddenly remembered the spring fling dance. That's right! Aaron was taking me as his date. If I spend more time with him, I won't have to think about Jake. Aaron was hot too so Jake's body will haunt me no more!

I wondered if Jake was still going to the dance since he wasn't chasing after Liliana anymore. I hoped not because I want to see as less of him as possible.

Stay the fuck away from my dreams Jake Morris, I thought to myself.

16

15. Tug of War

On the night of the dance, I got ready excitedly. I couldn't wait to see the shocked looks on people's faces when I show up with none other than THE Aaron Morris! I finally felt like a confident queen.

I put on the new dress I bought for this special occasion and paired it with some silver strappy heels. I checked myself out. Not bad. I'm sure Aaron would approve.

Liliana came out wearing a sexy silver sequin dress. And of course, she looked gorgeous as always.

"Oh, you are going?" I asked casually.

"Of course I'm going, why wouldn't I?" Liliana said irritably.

"Who with? I mean since Jake isn't taking you anymore," I asked.

"Yes he is," she said.

"He is!" I was shocked. "I thought you guys had that argument and he ditched you on the sidewalk and now you guys hate each other?" I exclaimed.

"Um, yea. I am still mad at him for that. But he promised to take me to the dance and it was too late to find another date. Besides, he is popular so I'd rather suck it up and show him off rather than going with some nobody," Liliana said.

Of course, the queen bee wants to hold on to her status even if it means swallowing her pride. What did I expect?

"And he agreed to take you still?" I asked.

15. TUG OF WAR

"Yup," she said.

I don't understand Jake sometimes. Scratch that, I don't understand him ever.

I had been avoiding Jake since the dream situation and I still wasn't sure if I was ready to face him. At least Aaron will be with me to distract me this time.

The doorbell rang. They were here! I thought and ran to open the door expecting Aaron standing there. My smile faltered as Jake stood in front of me, gazing at me intensely, looking mighty fine in his tuxedo. His eyes met mine then they started to trail down my body and stopped on my legs.

I cleared my throat. "Hey, Liliana is inside," I said.

He didn't say anything and kept staring at my body.

"Jake!" I snapped.

"Sorry. I got distracted. Didn't know you had such nice long legs because you hide them under those awful sweat pants," he smirked.

"Are you making fun of me? Because if you are, you better zip it," I made a face.

"What, no I am not. I was just…"

"Whoaa Jane! You look hot!" Aaron exclaimed behind him so Jake stopped talking.

I blushed. I've never been called hot before. Maybe I should dress up more often.

"Stop it, you!" I said. "You don't look too shabby yourself, sexy man." I flirted.

"I am serious. This dress really suits you and your make up looks great," Aaron complimented me and leaned over to kiss me.

I kissed him back but pulled away quickly as I felt Jake's burning gaze on us. Why was he staring at us so intensely?

Liliana walked in a few minutes later. "Hey boys," she flipped her hair and stared at them seductively making me roll my eyes until they hurt.

"Hey," Jake said dryly. What, no compliments? I was sure Jake would fall in love with her all over again and forget all about her bitchiness as soon as he laid his eyes on her wearing that sexy dress. I guess he was tougher than I thought.

"Ready to have a great night?" Aaron smirked.

I nodded. I was beyond ready.

Aaron and I moved with the music on the dance floor. He was a great dancer and I was having a grand ole' time. Did I mention the look on everyone's face when we walked in? It would take forever to pick up all of their jaws off the floor. I guess everyone expected Liliana to score one of the Morris brothers but not me, the quiet, invisible, plain Jane.

"Wow, you are a terrible dancer," Aaron said and laughed.

"Thanks a lot, jerk!" I laughed back. "I am only good at slow dances. But this is fun anyway," I said.

He nodded in agreement. I saw Jake dancing with Liliana at the corner of my eyes. He was looking directly at us and not paying attention to Liliana at all.

"What's up with Jake?" I whispered through the loud music.

"What do you mean?" he whispered back.

"Why is he acting all weird. He keeps staring at us like a creeper," I said.

"Maybe he is jealous that I get to dance with the hotter sister," Aaron offered.

"Hah, you flatter me," I said.

"I am not joking. You look really awesome, Jane," he said. His green eyes gazed into mine fondly.

"Thanks, it means a lot hearing you say that," I said. It really did. This was the first time in my life I wasn't overshadowed by Liliana's beauty. Someone actually noticed me!

The music shifted into the slower tune. It was time for the slow dance. Aaron grabbed my waist and pulled me closer to him. I put my arms around his neck and we swayed with the music slowly.

Someone tapped on my shoulder so we stopped dancing. "May I cut in?" Jake asked and grabbed my arm and pulled me towards him without waiting for Aaron's answer.

"Eh...we are in the middle of a romantic dance which you just interrupted,"

15. TUG OF WAR

Aaron said and grabbed my other arm.

"Well, it's my turn to dance with Janey," Jake insisted and pulled me towards him again.

"No, she is my date so she is dancing with me," Aaron insisted and pulled me to him again.

What the hell is going on? Why were the Morris brothers playing tug of war with me?

"Well, I saw her first so I have the right to dance with her," Jake pulled me a bit harder this time so I almost tumbled toward him.

"Jane is not an object and you aren't even friends. Stop bullying her. If she wanted to dance with you she would've said yes," Aaron glared at him and pulled me even harder.

Okay, I have to say something before I lose my arms.

"Guys, please, you will separate my arms from my body. Take it easy with all that pulling," I said desperately and laughed nervously. This is not how I planned to spend my night.

"Okay, let's ask her. Janey, would you like to dance?" Jake smirked. "Say yes or I will make you pay at school tomorrow," he leaned over and whispered sweet threats in my ears.

"Hey! Stop trying to intimidate her. Jane, you don't have to say yes if you don't want to," Aaron said.

"Um…I…I WANT FRUIT PUNCH!" I yelled and yanked my hands free then ran away.

17

16. I Don't Want to Dance

What the hell is going on? I mean what in the actual hell is happening? I always thought two boys fighting over me would be a dream come true but when it is happening for real, I want to run away to Canada and never look back. I mean, Aaron said it himself, I was a terrible dancer. So why are they both so obsessed over dancing with me? I don't understand.

I saw Liliana by the snack bar and strode over to her.

"You crazy hoe, did you put him up to this?" I grabbed her hand and yanked her towards me to get her attention.

"What are you talking about?" Liliana looked at me quizzically.

"I am talking about Jake, he was trying to force me to dance with him just now," I said. I was flustered from running away from the bad boy duo.

"Huh? Really? Why would he want to dance with you? He is my date," Liliana said.

"THAT'S WHAT I AM SAYING!" I yelled at her face. "Control your boy, lady," I said.

"Jesus Jane, just calm down. I just went to talk to some of the friends and when I came back he was gone. So he was over there trying to dance with you, huh?" Liliana said and looked at me curiously.

"Yes, and I need you to make him go away. Use your beauty to lure him away from me," I sighed.

16. I DON'T WANT TO DANCE

"I don't believe this," Liliana shook her head. "What do they see in you? First Aaron, now Jake? You couldn't be satisfied with one brother now you have to have both?" she said angrily.

"What are you saying! I never planned any of this. Aaron asked me out. And Jake…" I paused. "I am sure Jake is just trying to mess with me to make my life miserable. For some reason, he loves bullying me. Ever since we met, he wouldn't leave me alone," I pouted. "Please help me. You are my sister, goddammit!"

"Fine, I'll try," Liliana said and sighed. "Just go back to your stupid dance with Aaron."

I took a deep breath and headed back to the spot where I left the boys. Weirdly enough, they are still standing there. Most likely having a glaring contest.

"Hey, I am back. Oh look, the slow song is over so now I don't have to dance with either of you. Problem solved," I announced.

Aaron's eyes softened when he saw me. "I am sorry about my asshole brother, he doesn't take the hint and doesn't go away when he needs to," he said.

Jake reached out and grabbed my hand again. "I am not letting you get away yet. You are dancing with me, slow song or not," he said. He almost looked like a stubborn kid who is throwing a tantrum in a store to get the toy he wants. Is that what I am to him? A toy to play with?

Liliana showed up right then. "How about you dance with your date instead, Jake?" she cooed.

"Forget it, Liliana. You made it clear that you weren't interested in me before. I know you only wanted to come to the dance together to save your reputation so you can drop the whole cutesy act and leave me the fuck alone," Jake said and glared at her.

Ouch! Sis is getting rejected by the biggest man whore of our high school despite being extremely beautiful. That says something about her character.

Liliana looked like she got slapped in the face and stepped back. "Fuck you, Jake! No one wants to be with a jerk like you anyway!" she cried and stomped away.

"Well, that was pretty dramatic, Jake. But I am here with Aaron so please kindly leave us alone," I said. I've had enough of him at this point.

Jake stared at me intently. "This isn't over," he said in a low voice that sounded almost menacing. I am DOOMED.

Jake didn't bother us for the rest of the night. I saw him flirting with some blondes by the chocolate fountain. Good riddance. Aaron and I danced for a few songs then he drove me back home. I went to sleep feeling happy.

The next day at school, I found a note stuck inside my locker.

Meet me at our usual place by the fence after school or I will drag your ass out there myself.

Love Jake.

The note said.

Son of a bitch...what does he want now?

I didn't have the galls to ignore his request so I complied like a good girl. I went to see him after school.

He was leaned against the fence, smoking like a chimney. He dropped the cigarette as soon as he saw me approaching. I guess he remembered my asthma issue.

"I am here. What do you want, Jake?" I sighed.

He stepped towards me and gripped my hand so tightly it almost hurt.

"I didn't appreciate the way you treated me last night Janey," he said and looked at me coldly.

"The way I treated you? You were trying to force me to dance with you and I didn't want to. I don't have to do everything you ask me to, you know." I said.

"What, you are a brave girl all of a sudden just because you are going out with my brother now, is that it? You think you can defy me and there will be no consequences?" he sneered.

"You can't control me, Jake. You mean nothing to me. You aren't even my friend. I want you to leave me alone because you are just a bully!" I exclaimed. I am honestly getting tired of his attitude.

He grabbed my shoulder all of a sudden and pushed me against the fence, caging me in his arms so I can't get away. He then grabbed my chin with his

16. I DON'T WANT TO DANCE

thumb and lifted my face up, forcing me to look him in the eyes. He leaned closer. His lips were so close to my mouth that I thought he was going to kiss me but he whispered in my ears instead.

"I'll never leave you alone, Janey. You are mine to play with," he said.

"I am not your toy," I said and tried to sound confident but my voice came out meek and quiet.

"We'll see about that," he said. His voice was cold and harsh. I shivered. This was the Jake I was familiar with but he hadn't been this mean to me the last couple of days so I was not used to him acting evil.

He picked up a lock of my hair and ran his fingers through it. "About last night, since you decided to piss me off, get ready for your punishment," he smirked.

"P...punishment? What punishment?" I stammered.

"You just wait and see," he said.

"I'll tell Aaron, he would..." I tried it.

"You think I am scared of Aaron? He is my brother. I can handle him. Besides, he can't protect you at school since he doesn't go here anymore. You get to be stuck with me right here, eight hours a day so are you sure it's a good idea to get him involved and piss me off even more?" He asked and grinned.

Shit, he was right. Aaron can't save me from him when I am at school.

"I..I am leaving.." I said and pushed him off of me.

"Sure, no problem. Bye Janey. Can't wait to see you tomorrow," he gave me an evil smirk. That bastard.

18

17. Awaiting Punishment

A week went by but Jake didn't do or say anything to me. I was in a full panic mode. What did Jake have in store for me? What kind of punishment was he talking about? Ugh! I'm gonna go crazy!

I kept looking over my shoulders expecting something bad to happen. I even avoided stairs like he should push me down or something. I know I am being ridiculous but he is so intimidating!

I saw him in school several times but he never approached me or say anything to me. Maybe this was the punishment. Being afraid of the unknown. He was trying to mentally torture me to death!

I had math club after school so I didn't get home until 5 in the afternoon. I was relieved as the school was over and I got to avoid confrontation with Jake the whole day. I'm safe for now.

After I got home I decided to take a nice long hot shower then head to bed. All that anticipation of Jake torturing me made me exhausted.

My phone buzzed and there was a text from Aaron.

Hey cutie, what are you up to tonight? He texted.

Nothing, I'm going to bed early, I replied.

My phone buzzed again so I looked at Aaron's reply.

Awe, that's too bad. Maybe I will see you tomorrow? He said.

Yes, maybe , I hit send.

Tomorrow is the weekend so I should definitely go out with Aaron, I thought

17. AWAITING PUNISHMENT

to myself. It'll keep my mind off of Jake. Besides, being close to Aaron will keep me safe from Jake, I thought.

My phone buzzed again. Did Aaron send me more messages? I opened the text and almost dropped my phone. It was from Jake!

Don't think I forgot about you, my little Janey. Your punishment still awaits. He wrote.

Where did you get my number? I asked.

It wasn't hard to get. Your sister is pretty stupid. I can't believe I used to like her but mistakes happen, he text said.

Thanks a lot, Liliana. Now Jake get to harass me through texts too.

Why can't you leave me be? It's been a week since the dance. Let it go already! I typed furiously.

I didn't get any answer for a while. I wondered what he was thinking about.

Like mentioned before, I'll never leave you alone. So you should just embrace your new life as my plaything now, was his answer.

Aaaah! He is so infuriating! What did I ever do to deserve this? How would I ever get rid of him? Questions I didn't have the answers to. I threw my phone on the bed and headed inside the bathroom. Liliana was at her friend's house so I can shower as long as I wanted without her complaining.

The warm water poured down my head and my body and I instantly felt better. I'm going to forget all about Jake and his bullying for now. It's time to relax on my bed and watch Criminal Minds. Maybe I can learn how to murder Jake from the show.

I wrapped myself in a towel and stepped into my room.

"I've been waiting for you," A deep voice spoke from my bed.

I screamed as I saw Jake half laying on my bed with an evil smirk on his face.

"Aaaaaaah!" I screamed at the top of my lungs but no one heard it since no-one was home.

"Holy shit, must you screech like a banshee?" Jake scowled and covered his ears.

"What the fuck are you doing in my room, you...you pervert!" I yelled.

"Chill out! I didn't know you were gonna come out all wet and half-naked. Although, I'm not exactly complaining," he grinned.

Ladies and gentlemen, today is the day I am going to prison for murdering Jake Morris.

"Did...did you break in?" I gasped.

"Yeap I had to. No one was home and I didn't feel like waiting," Jake shrugged.

"You have issues," I announced and gripped my towel so it doesn't fall off. I felt naked as Jake stared at me despite the towel that was covering half of my body.

He had a weird look on his face. The kind of look a wolf would give to its prey before eating it. In other words, I might be in trouble.

"You better get out of here before I start screaming again," I threatened him.

Jake jumped up and walked towards me slowly. "Go ahead and scream. Then see what happens," he said quietly and moved another inch towards me.

This was dangerous. I was alone with a horny teenage boy in my bath towel. How do I get out of this?

"Why are you here?" I repeated my question.

"Well you see Janey, I wanted to find something incriminating against you so I could use it to punish you, and I think I found the perfect material," he said.

"Wha...what did you find?" I asked nervously.

He went over to my bed and shoved his hand under the pillow.

Oh no, I know what he was talking about now.

He took out my prized possession, the lockbox for my most innermost secrets. My freaking diary.

Just go ahead and kill me now.

"No Jake! Put that back! That's private." I cried.

"Nope. In order to punish you, I'm going to read some of your deep dark secrets, out loud," he said and gave me an evil smile. What did I say? He is the spawn of Satan.

"You can't!" I gripped my towel with one hand and tried to grab the diary

17. AWAITING PUNISHMENT

with the other. But he stood up and held it over his head so I couldn't reach it.

"Let's see... let's start with the latest entry, shall we?" he said and opened it.

No way, that's the one where I wrote about my wet dream!

"Dear diary, last night I had the craziest dream. I was with..." he proceeded to read some more, but before he could get to the part where I get it on with him, I did the only thing I could think of doing in order to stop him from reading. I dropped my freaking towel.

Jake stopped in his track and stared at my body. He dropped the diary on the floor and continued to stare at my boobs. His eyes were huge with shock.

"Um...Jane.." he cleared his throat.

I quickly grabbed the diary off the floor.

"Hah! I got it! I won't let you read it now, you imbecile!" I cried.

"It's okay, I'd rather look at those," he said and pointed at my chest, still looking shocked.

Look at what...oh....no... what the hell did I just do?

19

18. Get Out of My Room!

Oh no oh no oh no. Why did I do this? Why? This is the best you could do to distract him? Really Jane?

The next few seconds went in slow motion. I was so embarrassed that I wanted dig a hole and die. And it was my own fault for being a dumbass.

"Y...you...I can't believe you'd rather have me see you naked than let me read your diary. Un fucking believable," Jake shook his head and burst into laughter.

"Ugh! I don't know! It's all your fault. You pushed me too far. You are so cruel, I hate you!" I screamed which turned into sobs. Tears started to fall down my cheeks before I could control them. I hated my body, now Jake saw it. He saw all of it!

Jake looks like he was taken aback by my outburst. He quickly picked up the blanket from my bed and ran towards me then covered me up.

"Hey, stop that. Why are you crying?" he said awkwardly. This shouldn't make him feel uncomfortable because he makes people cry all time, right?

"B...because, you saw me naked. I don't like people to look at my body," I sniffled.

"Jesus..." he muttered under his breath. He looked at me again. His eyes were dark but they didn't look cold this time. "I didn't see anything so stop crying," he tried to reassure me.

"Yes you did! You stared right at it. And I know you are going to make fun

18. GET OUT OF MY ROOM!

of it now," I said and looked down.

"Why would I make fun of it you weirdo? You have such pretty boo...I mean I don't know because I didn't see anything. So I won't," he said quickly.

I wiped my tears and looked up. "Really?" I asked hopefully.

"Yes. Except for the part where you did this so I don't read your stupid diary. It's too ridiculous. I'm probably gonna make fun of you for that for the rest of your life," he smirked.

I smiled. "Do your worst, jerk," I said. I was already feeling better. Jake didn't look all that disgusted by my body so that's good I guess.

"You've peaked my interest now. What's in that diary that is so important?" he looked at me curiously.

"Eh...you don't need to know. Secrets obviously," I let out an awkward laugh.

"I bet you wrote dirty things about me in there, which is why you can't let me see it," he said casually.

"Whaa...no way! I like Aaron, remember? I can't stand you," I shook my head no.

"Are you sure? Then tell me why do you like him?" he asked, turning serious again.

"He is better looking and nicer and a better kisser...I mean my guess is he is a better kisser but I wouldn't know but I'm guessing it's true because, you are an asshole and you suck! I announced

"Oh yeah? Let's test out that theory, shall we?" he grinned.

"Huh? What are you talking about?" I didn't like where I this was going.

" Let's see who the better kisser is," he kept walking toward me until my back was against the wall. He trapped me between his arms and leaned closer to my face.

"Jake, stop messing around," I said with shaky breath.

He cupped my cheeks and stared at me intensely then smashed his lips against mine.

A fire ignited inside of me when Jake started kissing me. He sucked on my lower lips, then his insistent mouth slowly parted my trembling lips, which sent wild goosebumps all over my body. The heat rose in my cheeks as his tongue slipped inside of my mouth, gently at first, but then it became demanding.

Jake Morris is kissing me, my inner thought shouted.

I let go of the blanket without even realizing it and put my hands on his chest to grip his shirt. He moved fast and grabbed the blanket before it fell on the ground which he then tightly wrapped around my body and held it so it would stay in its place. This boy can be weirdly considerate sometimes, I thought.

My hands automatically gripped his hair and I pulled him closer to kiss him back. My entire body felt hot and tingly. He tilted my head and deepened the kiss as if I wasn't having a hard time breathing already. I moaned in his mouth. Is he trying to suffocate me with this kiss?

Jake Morris is kissing me and I was kissing him back like a hungry beast, the reality hit me again and I screamed internally.

I felt something hard between my legs and my eyes snapped open. I broke the kiss immediately.

"Jake...wha...what..." I could barely form a sentence as my mind went completely blank. He was still holding on to me. I could hear his heart thumping against his chest.

"Mm...you taste just like I imagined," he practically growled in my ears.

"Y...you...what you mean you imagined?" I stammered. "Since when?" I could hardly recognize my own voice as it sounded breathy and whispery.

"It doesn't matter since when. What matters is that I want you. And judging from the way you responded, it is safe to say that you want me too," he smirked.

I didn't know what I wanted. I felt so confused. On one hand, I felt like I had feelings for Aaron, and on the other...

"We shouldn't be doing this. I am supposed to be going out with Aaron. He actually likes me. And you, you just want to play with me!" I exclaimed.

"That's not what I am doing," Jake protested.

"Then what are you doing? You told me yesterday I was your plaything, didn't you?" I said and backed away from him.

Those were his exact words at school so excuse me for not trusting him

18. GET OUT OF MY ROOM!

right away. I have been dissed by people too many times to fall in his feet just because we shared a passionate kiss.

He went quiet at first. His eyes gazed into mine for the longest time. "Yeah, I said that but..."

"But what Jake? Just because you are a great kisser I am supposed to jump into your lap? You don't care about me. You just want to get laid," I cried.

"Is that what you think what's happening?" he sneered at me. His demeanor suddenly turned dark. "You think I just kissed you because I want to fuck you? But so what if I do? Don't try to pretend like you don't want me," he pointed out.

"I am not going to deny the attraction I am feeling toward you but that doesn't mean I'll let you have me whenever you want either. You don't even think I am pretty. You called me plain Jane remember? I am not going to be another girl you use and throw away," I said. My eyes started to tear up but I didn't care.

"You know what Jane if that's what you think of me then so be it. I don't give a fuck. You don't know what the hell you want so when you figure it out, come find me," Jake said angrily and proceeded to climb down the window.

"You can use the front door, you know," I yelled.

"Fuck your front door and fuck your insecurities!" Jake yelled back while climbing.

"That was uncalled for you asswipe! I am not insecure!" I yelled out the window but he was already gone.

I sighed knowing that Jake was right. I was letting my insecurities get in the way of my desires. But how can I trust a guy who only dated the most beautiful and voluptuous girls in our school? I couldn't let myself get carried away and end up getting my heart broken and that's the fact.

20

19. The Confession

At school, I saw Jake but he just ignored me. I guess I made him very angry this time.

I couldn't stop thinking about our kiss. I've never thought someone would kiss me like that. It was so passionate and so...hot. My entire body shook with awareness every time I remember how soft his lips felt and the way his tongue caressed the inside of my mouth. Ugh, who knew a kiss could turn me on this much and make a mess of me. I wanted more.

Screw you, Jake, for making me feel this way, I thought.

I guess I should be relieved since the whole ordeal drove Jake away from me. He was ignoring me instead of bothering me now. But why do I feel this pressure in my heart?

I saw him hanging out with Jenny Patterson at the cafeteria. Our eyes met for a brief second but he just glared at me and brought his attention back to Jenny. He picked up a lock of her hair and twirled it around in a flirty manner.

Jealousy welled up inside of me. That bastard was purposely trying to hurt me now!

I saw him leaning down and what it looks like, kissing her neck. Oh hell no...

I picked up my pizza on a tray and strode over to their direction. I pretended to go to the table behind him but on the way to the table, I purposely tripped and dropped the entire slice of pizza on top of Jenny's head.

"Ugh! Gross! What the hell is the matter with you!" she squealed.

19. THE CONFESSION

"Oh nooo! your shiny golden locks! Oopsie, my bad," I feigned shock and gasped and kept walking.

Okay, I'll admit it. That was totally mean and unnecessary toward Jenny. She is just a poor, innocent girl who happened to like my Jake.

Wait, did I just call him *my* Jake? I must've gone insane.

Jenny ran off to wash her hair so I just kept walking until I disappeared from Jake's view, but not before I caught him staring at me intently. Did he suspect me? But I didn't want to wait and find out.

When the school was over, I went to see Aaron since I promised him I'd hang out with him. We went to a fast-food restaurant to grab some lunch. I felt guilty being here with him after that kiss with Jake. But at the same time, it's not like Jake and my relationship would go anywhere anyway.

"Are you okay?" Aaron asked.

"Yeah...sorry I just got distracted, you were saying?" I said. My mind was still filled with the thoughts of Jake.

"Nothing, you wanna get out of here?" he asked.

"Yeah sure. Where?" I asked.

"How about my house? We haven't had any alone time since the dance," he said.

"Um..okay," I agreed distractedly.

I regretted coming to his house as soon as I arrived. What if I run into Jake? He lived here too. Ugh, why did they have to be brothers?

"I really like you, Jane, I think you are a great girl," Aaron said after a moment.

"Ehh...thank you, you are pretty amazing yourself," I said awkwardly.

Aaron chuckled. "I am glad you think so," he said and leaned in to kiss me.

I suddenly felt guilty. I couldn't deceive Aaron like this. Even if nothing is going on between Jake and me, Aaron deserved to know the truth.

"Wait I can't. I have to tell you something," I said.

"What is it?" his eyes were full of worry.

"I...well...Jake..." I could find the right words.

"What about Jake? Did he do something to you? I swear I am gonna kil-..."

"We kissed!" I couldn't hold it anymore.

"Sorry what?" Aaron asked.

"J..Jake kissed me the other night and I kissed him back," I repeated.

Aaron didn't say anything for a moment. Maybe my sudden outburst rendered him speechless. I wouldn't blame him if he gets angry at me and never speaks to me again.

"I am really sorry Aaron," I said.

"So, do you like Jake?" he asked.

"Honestly? I don't know. He confuses me. He was the one who made a move on me. I should've pushed him away. I should've smacked him for planting that kiss on me without a warning but I just couldn't," I said.

"I told you he liked you Jane, but you didn't believe me," Aaron shook his head.

"I still don't believe it!" I cried. "I am pretty sure he is just trying to mess with my head, trying to get a rise out of me," I said.

"Why would you think that?" Aaron asked.

"Do you really have to ask? You know how he is! He changes girlfriends like socks if it even gets that far. What if he just wants to use me for sex? I couldn't do it, I refuse to," I declared.

"Yeah I get that," he agreed. "Is that it?" he asked.

"What do you mean?" I looked at him quizzically.

"A kiss? That's all you did?" Aaron asked.

"Y...yeah?" I hesitated. I couldn't tell him about the burning passion I felt from that heated kiss. It felt a lot more than just a kiss.

"I guess then don't worry about it. Just get past it and move on," Aaron shrugged.

"What? That's it? Aren't you mad?" I asked.

"Of course I am a little mad. But I really like you, Jane. I am not gonna just give up on you," he grinned.

I was a little taken aback by his declaration. Not exactly the reaction I expected from him. But then again, Aaron was also popular with girls when he was in high school. Maybe that's why he doesn't think a kiss is a big deal.

"What about Jake?" I asked.

"What about him? Did he ask you out?" Aaron looked at me curiously.

19. THE CONFESSION

"No…after I told him I didn't want to move any farther, he got mad at me and left me alone," I said.

"Then he is no threat to me. Besides, he is my brother. He had always been impulsive and temperamental. He probably kissed you on a whim and forgot about it once it was over. So don't worry about him," Aaron said.

Easy for him to say that. Even if it didn't mean anything to Jake, it meant something to me. But if Jake doesn't want anything to do with me I have no choice but to try and move past it.

"I guess you are right," I said quietly.

Aaron leaned forward and cupped my cheek. "I can tell you aren't fully into me yet but don't worry, I'll win you over," he said and gazed into my eyes with those intense green eyes of his. I didn't realize he was that serious about me and that scared me a little. Something told me I don't want Aaron to get angry.

But what about how I felt with Jake? How can I just forget about it?

21

20. Are You a Vampire?

I should feel relieved as Aaron was so nice about the whole thing but I still felt an ache in my heart. Something just felt wrong. Why couldn't I get Jake out of my mind? It was just one stupid kiss and it didn't even mean anything to him.

My phone buzzed all of a sudden so I checked my text messages.

Meet me in the park by your house, Jake texted me.

Ugh...what does he want now?

Why? I replied.

Stop asking stupid questions and just show up already, he texted. Only Jake can sound so aggressive through texts. I rolled my eyes.

Fine, I'll play his game. I headed to the park. It was getting colder so I zipped up my hoodie and put the hood on. I shouldn't have worn shorts, I thought as I shivered slightly.

Jake was sitting on the swing, looking at his phone. The wind must've messed up his hair because it looked a lot more messy and wild which for some reason made him look even more handsome.

His eyes lit up and his lips twisted into a smirk when he saw me approaching.

"Janey, you came," he said.

"I just didn't feel like dealing with your threats and intimidation today," I said.

"You act like that's all I do to you. All the time," he frowned.

20. ARE YOU A VAMPIRE?

"You are kidding, right? YES! You do that to me a lot more than you think," I snapped.

"Whatever," he shrugged.

I don't know what I expected from him. An apology? Jake would never.

"Why did you ask me to come here?" I asked. It was getting colder and I wanted to go home.

"Today at the cafeteria, why did you do that thing to Jenny?" he asked. He had an amused expression on his face.

"What, the pizza thing? That was just an accident," I said. The hell it was.

"Don't give me that bullshit Janey, I know what an accident looks like. That sure as hell didn't look like one. I have been watching you and I saw you trip on purpose," he smirked.

"You were watching me? What were you watching me for?" I countered.

"Don't try to change the subject. You were jealous weren't you?" he pressed.

"No way!" I protested.

"You were jealous I was paying so much attention to Jenny and you wish it was you I was doing it to," he continued.

"I don't want to listen to this bullcrap. I am leaving," I said and attempted to walk away but he grabbed my hand and enclosed it inside his fist.

"Let go.." I whispered.

"Not until you admit you want me," Jake stared at me hard. His eyes were dark and determined.

"No. I don't want you, I don't care about you," my voice shook as I tried to convince myself of what I just claimed.

"You are such a liar," he whispered and grazed my lips with his thumb. I shivered, but this time, it was not from the cold.

"Janey, Janey, Janey. What am I gonna do with you? you make me lose my fucking mind," he whispered and moved closer to me.

"I don't know what you are talking about," I said and closed my eyes as he started to caress my cheeks. His fingers felt warm and rough against my skin.

He grabbed my waist and pulled me closer.

He leaned forward and kissed my mouth that I parted without even thinking. His mouth tasted hot and sweet like he had been eating a candy bar. He firmly held on to my hips and pushed my body against him so I don't run away from him. I felt my heart flutter even though the kiss lasted for only 10 seconds.

"What are you so afraid of?" he asked.

"You," I replied. My eyes were closed as I still felt the sensation from his touches.

"You don't trust me," Jake said and ran his fingers through my hair.

I didn't say anything. I needed to get away from him because it was impossible to form coherent thoughts when he was touching me like this.

I pulled myself away from him. "I told Aaron about us kissing. He still wants to be with me so I want you to leave me alone," I said weakly.

Anger flickered in his dark brown eyes. "Why are you being so stubborn? I told you you belong to me, Jane. Do you think I'll let you off that easily? Look at you! You melt in my arms every time I touch you. You want me!"

"Why me? You have all these girls you can choose from? What's so special about me. Is it because I look like some average weak girl who will listen to your ridiculous demands. So you can control me?" I cried.

"You think I'm that horrible, huh?" he let out a frustrated laugh.

"Well, that's how you act, so... " I said.

"I'm not going to stand here and try to defend myself to you. I don't owe you shit. I just came here because I missed you," he smirked.

"Fuck you," I sneered at him.

"That's the goddamn plan," he laughed.

Ugh...he is so infuriating.

He wrapped his arms around me all of a sudden and pressed his mouth on my neck before I could make a move. I shivered as I felt him nibbling on my skin and whelped as I felt a soft bite.

"Ah! What the hell are you doing?" I squealed.

"Marking you, since you are too stubborn to leave Aaron," he said and continued to lick and nibble my neck.

"Stop that! You aren't a vampire," I giggled as it was starting to tickle.

"Mmm...almost done," he smiled against my skin and continued. He stepped back to admire his handiwork. "There, have fun explaining that to him."

20. ARE YOU A VAMPIRE?

"I'm leaving," I announced and started to walk away.

"I'll walk you home shorty," he said and put his arms around my shoulders and started to walk with me. I rolled my eyes but let him keep me company.

I face planted on my pillow in frustration. I touched my neck. It felt tender so I went to look in the mirror to see what he did to it.

I gasped as I stared at the angry hickey he left me on my skin. No amount of concealer will cover this properly.

I hate him so much.

22

21. Pink Haired Nightmare

Jake teased me relentlessly for the next couple of days at school. Everywhere I went, he was there, flashing me his stupid boyish grin. He knocked the books out of my hands and kept walking one time. Ugh..how does he always figure out where I am?

All of his attention towards me made other girls jealous. I found them glaring at me from across the hall from time to time. Great...I just went from being invisible to the biggest rival of Jake's fangirls. Fuck my life.

I went to the restroom and while I washed my hands, a girl approached me. She was tall and skinny with bright pink hair and a beautiful face. She was wearing a low cut top that threatened the school code with straight-legged jeans. I recognized her as one of the seniors.

"Hey, I need to talk to you," she said.

Weird, she never tried to talk to me before. "Um...okay, what about?" I asked.

"I am Mayra. You are Jane Brown right?" she asked.

"Yes," I said.

"Well Jane, I came here to tell you that you need to stay away from Jake," Mayra said and stared at me with cold, hard eyes.

Oh great, I made an enemy.

"It'd be my pleasure," I said.

21. PINK HAIRED NIGHTMARE

She looked even angrier somehow. "Are you trying to fuck with me? Because I'm being completely serious. If you don't leave him alone I'd be forced to pluck out the hair off of your head," she threatened me.

"That would be really hard, my hair is too thick," I said casually.

"Bitch," she said with gritted teeth. "I don't see why he is so obsessed with you. You aren't even pretty!" she exclaimed.

You and me both sis.

"Look, Mayra, it's not what it looks like. I don't like him. In fact, I want him to leave me alone but he wouldn't stop bothering me. Why don't you go pluck *his* hair out?" I suggested.

Mayra didn't look amused but softened her tone of voice. "Jake is not what you think he is. You are probably loving all this attention because he is good looking and sexy but he is not a good person. He will hurt you just like he did others."

"Were you not listening to me? I don't *love* his attention at all. I wish he would leave me alone," I said again.

"That's what they all say at first then end up going to bed with him anyway," Mayra said.

Jeez....just how many girls did he seduce already?

"If you don't believe me go ask Emily Johnson. She is his latest conquest. I bet that's why he is after you. You are probably a virgin like her. Am I right? Jake LOVES virgins," Mayra chuckled.

Oh boy, I did declare my virginity to him once. What if this Mayra chick is on to something?

"What's it to you?" I asked.

"He did the same to me! He slept with me then ditched me. He said we can be friends but that's not what I want. I love Jake, he is going to be mine eventually," Mayra said.

"Well, good luck with everything. If that's all I'd like to go to my class now," I said irritably.

"Just remember what I told you. Steer clear of him or you will regret it," Mayra warned for one last time and left.

I sighed. Being harassed by Jake wasn't enough so now I have to deal with this pink-haired nightmare.

I was not going to let this whole bathroom situation slide. I decided to find Jake after school. I knew he hung out by that fence behind the building to smoke so I stormed over there.

"Awe Janey! I didn't even have to chase you down this time. You came to find me, did you miss me, baby?" Jake cooed and tried to kiss my cheek but I pushed his face away.

"Save it, pretty boy. I came to ask you, why is the human reincarnation of my little pony threatening me over you?" I demanded answers.

"Huh?" Jake was utterly confused.

"That pink-haired vixen, what's her name...Moira?" I asked.

"Oh you mean Mayra, she threatened you?" Jake asked.

"Yes, something about not to stand in line to become your conquest or I lose my hair," I said. "Not that I care anyway, my hair sucks," I added.

"I love your hair, so wild and cute," Jake smirked and ruffled my hair.

"FOCUS! My point is I don't want to be jumped by one of your fangirls. I am not good at girl fights. It's not like I want to sleep with you anyway," I said.

"Are you sure about that? That's not what it seems like. The way your body responds when I touch you tells me it wants more from me," he smirked.

"As if! Just tell her to stay away from me. And you stay away from me too!" I cried.

"Not gonna happen. And what was it about conquest? Why do you keep saying that?" he asked and looked at me curiously.

"She told me about you sleeping with girls and ditching them. She also told me you like to take girls' virginity," I said.

"She told you all that, huh?" he smiled but didn't deny it. The jerk...

"What else did she tell you?" he asked.

"She told me about Emily Johnson and what you did to her," I said.

His eyes went dark all of a sudden. "There are two sides to every story," he said quietly.

"Mayra also told me that, she was one of the girls you slept with and then friend-zoned her. And...she is in love with you," I said.

21. PINK HAIRED NIGHTMARE

"I can't help it if girls fall for me. It's not my job to coddle every girl's heart," he shrugged.

"You arrogant, self preening asshole. And you wonder why I don't trust you," I shook my head in disappointment.

"You are different," he said.

"No, I am not. She is probably right. I bet I am suddenly alluring to you because I told you I was a virgin. Well, I am not going to let you take it!" I declared.

"Jesus Jane, stop believing everything people say to you. I am telling you I like you more than everyone else. I don't care if you are a virgin or not. How else can I prove it to you?" Jake said in a frustrated manner.

"Just...leave me alone and keep Mayra away from me too. Goodbye," I said and proceeded to make my dramatic exit.

"Janey..."

"I SAID GOODBYE TO YOU SIR!" I yelled and ran off. Ain't nobody got time for Jake's bullfuckery.

23

22. Parties are Not Fun

"A party?" I looked at Aaron questioningly. "Whose party?"

"One of my old friends from high school. His sister is in your grade so you might see people you know too," Aaron said.

"Oh okay," I wasn't particularly excited. I never liked going to social gatherings. I always ended up standing against a well and watch other people have fun. Not exactly my type of fun.

"Don't worry, it'll be fun," Aaron reassured me. Will it though?

So I started to get ready for the said party. It was a Saturday night and I had nothing to do anyway. I borrowed one of Liliana's dress. Well more like blackmailed her into giving it to me. I had no cute clothes. Usually, I didn't care how I looked but things are different now. I didn't want to look like a bum next to a stud like Aaron. I've got a reputation to maintain.

I put on a red body-con dress. I lined my eyes with some eyeliners then lightly glossed my lips. I let my hair down and curled it into loose waves. I checked the mirror and admired myself a bit. Not bad for a plain Jane.

Aaron came to pick me up. He checked me out and smiled in approval. His eyes reflected lust which made me feel shy and flustered.

"Wow, you surprise me every time I see you," he smirked.

"I am bag full of shockers. So, who is your friend? I mean who is throwing the party?" I asked.

"Ricky Elliot," he said.

22. PARTIES ARE NOT FUN

Oh, I vaguely remember Ricky. He was in cahoots with Aaron throughout high school. I wondered if he quit his bad-boy ways like Aaron. I doubted it.

We arrived at the party shortly. I paused when I entered the living room when I spotted Jake sitting on the couch. A girl practically sat on his lap. It was none other than Miss Pink-haired vixen. I guess she had won after all. Sneaky biatch. I felt a little jealous.

"Oh great...Jake is here too," I remarked.

"He won't do anything to you. I'll make sure of it," Aaron said gruffly. Well, I sure hope so, I thought.

Mayra was whispering something in Jake's ear but he looked like he had zero interest in listening to her. But he wasn't exactly pushing her off of his lap either. He is such a slut. But I wasn't surprised.

Just as I was about to tell Aaron to go to a different room, Jake looked at my direction and our eyes met. His eyes scanned my body from head to toe. He kept looking at me but didn't smile or say anything. But I acknowledged the look on his face. Lust.

"Um..can we go somewhere else?" I asked Aaron as Jake's lusty eyes were making me uncomfortable. I blushed.

"Yeah, let's go introduce you to Ricky," he said and took my hand and pulled me away.

Ricky eyed me for a moment and grinned. "Yeah, I remember you from high school. Your sister is pretty hot," he said.

"Yeah I know," I rolled my eyes.

"I don't remember you looking this fine though, you've blossomed," he smirked.

Ewe...who says stuff like this? Gross.

"Thanks. I guess," I replied.

Jake came into the room all of a sudden. "Oh, hey bro. Nice of you to take my girl out on a date," he said.

"She is not your girl. Keep dreaming little brother," Aaron smirked.

Oh god, not this again. "I am going to the bathroom while you two sort this out," I sighed and left them behind.

As I was looking in the mirror and fixing my hair, someone burst in. It was

Mayra.

"YOU! I thought I told you to stay away from Jake," she cried and pointed at me.

"In case you haven't noticed, I am here with Aaron, not Jake" I said irritably.

"Then why did Jake push me away as soon as you entered the room?" she demanded to know.

"Heck if I know? Why don't you go ask him?" I said. I felt a tinge of happiness despite of everything. Did Jake push her away because of me?

"I am not playing games with you anymore you little bitch. You will pay for getting in my way. BOYS! Get in here!" she cried.

Two guys came in and grabbed me.

24

23. This is not a Threesome

I tried to scream but one of the guys pressed his palm on my mouth to muffle the noise. The other one picked up my legs then they proceeded to carry me somewhere.

"Have fun guys! I bet Jake won't want you if you are not a virgin!" Mayra yelled out and laughed.

I tried to struggle out of their grasps but failed miserably. They took me inside a room and dropped me on the bed.

"Mayra said you were ugly but I think you are pretty fucking hot, don't you agree Mike?" one of the guys grinned and said it to the other guy.

"Yeah, she ain't half bad," Mike chuckled.

"Guys, there must be some kind of misunderstanding. I don't know what Mayra told you but I am not trying to steal Jake from her," I said desperately and looked around frantically. I don't know how I am going to get out of this situation.

"Frankly, We don't give a fuck what's going on between you and that pink-haired bitch. We just want some pussy," Mike said and hovered over me.

I flinched in disgust as I smelled alcohol in his breath. I tried to push him off by placing both of my hands on his chest then kicked him.

"FUCK! You bitch!" he screamed and slapped me. "Hold her legs, Tank."

What kind of name is Tank? Anyway, now is not the time to ponder on that.

"NOOO! Get off of me!" I screamed and tried to hit him but he pinned my arms down.

"Now let's get this hot little dress off of you so we can start having some fun," Mike said in a menacing tone and tried to take off my dress.

This isn't good. I couldn't let them defile me, I couldn't!

Tears started to stream down my face as Mike ripped the bottom of my dress and pull down my underwear. But before he could go any farther, the door broke open and Aaron stormed in, followed by Jake.

YES! My heroes! I thought in my head. Thank you, God.

"GET THE FUCK OFF OF OUR GIRLFRIEND!" Aaron roared.

I am sorry, did Aaron just said 'our girlfriend'? I am gonna have to talk to him about that later.

Mike was startled but didn't get off me immediately. Tank let go of my legs and stood up straight and looked at the Morris brothers with fear in his eyes.

"Err...Aaron and Jake? What are you guys doing here?" Mike asked innocently.

"Care to explain why you are on top of Jane with your dick hanging out?" Jake gritted his teeth. His face was red and his eyes were glowing with rage. I fear for Mike and Tank's well beings.

"Mayra told us to! She said Jane wanted to try threesome so we are just helping out," Tank let out a nervous chuckle. This lying sack of shit.

"Is that right? Because it looks like to me, you are forcing yourselves on Jane," Aaron said and grabbed Tank's shirt then punched him directly on his nose. Tank yelped like a dying puppy and fell on the floor.

"Your turn now bitch," Jake said and kicked Mike on the stomach. Then he grabbed his collar and punched his face.

"Fuck! I am sorry! I swear I won't touch her again," Mike started to cry as Jake proceeded to kick him again.

Aaron kicked Tank again a few more times until he bled while Jake did a number on Mike. While I didn't condone violence, this was satisfying to watch.

Jake ran to me after he was done with Mike. He lifted me up and wrapped his arms tightly around me.

"Janey, are you okay?" he asked quietly.

23. THIS IS NOT A THREESOME

His hug was so warm and comforting and his voice was so sweet that I couldn't hold it in anymore. I started to cry hysterically.

Aaron ran up to us and crouched down then stroked my hair. "Shh...it's okay. We wouldn't let anyone hurt you," he said gently.

I kept my face buried in Jake's shirt and let it all out. I am going to have to buy him a new shirt later.

He let go of me and looked at Aaron. "Take care of her for a minute, I'll be right back," he said.

Aaron nodded and hugged me. "Are you hurt?" he asked.

"Not physically but, I was so scared," I whispered.

"I know sweetheart, we'll make sure those guys never come near you again," Aaron promised and kissed me on the forehead.

Jake came in a moment later, dragging Mayra with him. He threw her on the floor in front of me.

"Jake what the hell?" she screeched.

"Apologize to Jane, RIGHT FUCKING NOW!" Jake roared. Mayra flinched.

"I have nothing to apologize for," Mayra pouted.

"You think I am some kind of an idiot? I know you told those guys to rape her. What kind of a girl does shit like that to another girl? Apologize before I lose my temper," Jake snarled.

"You better do it Mayra before I get involved too," Aaron threatened her with a fire in his eyes.

Mayra stood up and looked at me fearfully. "I am sorry Jane, I got jealous and acted stupid on impulse," she said.

"You can shove that apology up your fake butt," I glared at her.

"Alright, now kneel down in front of Jane while she smacks you on the face," Jake ordered.

"What! Jake, you aren't serious!" Mayra whined.

"Oh, he is pretty serious," Aaron said.

"I would do it myself but since I am a gentleman I am not gonna hit you. But Janey earned the right, so chop, chop, get on your knees," Jake said impatiently.

"But...Jake..." Mayra protested.

"I am gonna count to 5, do it by then or I'll be really pissed," Jake sneered.

"I would do it if I were you, Mayra, Jake gets ugly when he is pissed," Aaron smirked.

"1...2...3...4..." Jake started to count.

"Okay, okay!" Mayra screamed and knelt in front of me.

"Now, Jane, don't hold back and swing like a champion," Aaron suggested.

I got this.

"Jane, please...don't hit my face," Mayra pleaded.

I cracked my knuckles. "I am sorry Mayra but that pink dye had gotten inside your brain and turned you into a dumb bimbo. You should've left me alone," I said and smacked her on the face with all of my strength.

Mayra toppled over and laid on the floor with her palm pressed against her cheek. I hope it hurts more in the morning.

"Let's get you home," Aaron said.

Three of us went outside to his car.

"Thank you guys for everything, you really saved me today," I said and looked at them appreciatively.

"Of course, we would do anything for our girl," Jake smirked.

There it is again. "What do you mean by *our* girl?" I looked at them quizzically.

Aaron and Jake exchanged a look among themselves. Aaron cleared his throat and looked at me.

"Well...about that, Jake and I talked about it and none of us could agree on who should date you because none of us want to give up on you," he said.

"And?" I asked.

"So we decided both of us will date you now," Jake replied and gave me his boyish grin.

Um....excuse me....pretty boy duo said what now!?

25

24. I Don't Want This Fantasy

"What do you mean both of you will date me now?" I stared at them wide eyes. What kind of weird situation is this?

"I mean, you can date us both until you decide which one of us you like the best," Aaron said.

I was absolutely mortified by their preposterous proposal. I looked at them back and forth to see if they were being serious. None of them were laughing. What kind of girl do they take me for?

"I am sorry, am I being punked?" I asked, still trying to process what just happened.

"Look, Janey, I like you a lot and so does Aaron. And I also love my brother so I don't want to fight him over this. So this is the only way," Jake said.

"You two are out of your mind! What about me? You can't just decide that for me! I am not some toy you get to pass around, you jerks," I cried. The audacity of these two.

"I am sorry Jane but we don't think of you as an object. We just both want a chance to be close to you. And we refuse to give up on you," Aaron looked at me intently.

"I know you like me, Jane, I don't care how many times you deny it but I can see it in your eyes. So I'll wait till you admit it then you'll be all mine," Jake said.

I am speechless. What kind of situation is this?

"I didn't agree with Jake at first, but I feel like you like him too but you also like me so I'll use it as an opportunity to make you mine," Aaron said.

"But wouldn't you get jealous if I go out with Jake?" I pointed out.

"Of course I will. But I'll get over it for now," he said.

"Same here. I get angry every time Aaron goes near you but I'll leave it up to you on what you want to do," Jake said.

I am going to scream.

"That is the dumbest thing I've ever heard but I am too tired to deal with this now so just take me home," I sighed.

"Yes ma'am!" Aaron smirked.

He drove me home in silence. Both of them got out of the car to see me off.

"I am sorry about what happened today Jane, are you sure you are okay?" Aaron asked gently.

I nodded. "Thank you for what you did for me. Both of you," I smiled.

"You are precious to me, Janey. One day I'll convince you that you are not just some girl I want to fuck," Jake said.

My heart fluttered. I said goodbye to both of them and went inside. This has been the craziest night of my life. They are both being so amazing to me, how will I ever choose between them?

Aaron was sweet and he decided to not be a bully so he is a good person. He was also super hot with his sparkling green eyes and amazing smile. I really like him and think he genuinely wants to be with me.

Jake on the other hand was the most confusing guy I've ever met. One day he is the biggest asshole I know, the next he is being sweet to me. He was also super hot with his intense dark brown eyes and he had an amazing smile too. And the sexual attraction I felt towards him was strong. But I still didn't know if he wanted something serious with me or he was just trying to win me over to compete with his brother.

Ugh...I am so confused!

The next few days were disastrous. Jake flirted with me at school. Continuously and relentlessly. He simply wouldn't leave me alone. I felt like I was stuck in some 90s chick flick. You know the kind where two guys dared to date the same girl? Yes, I am that girl.

24. I DON'T WANT THIS FANTASY

Luckily, Aaron didn't go to school with us so at least I was safe from him for 8 hours. But he was always texting me and asking me to hangout.

I mean...don't get me wrong. I didn't entirely hate the situation. Two hot guys chasing after plain ole Jane while other girls in school burn from jealousy?

Is this supposed to be a beautiful dream or a nightmare?

26

25. Chasing Virgins

"Ahh, Jake! You are going to squeeze me to death!" I yelped and struggled but his arms tightened around me.

"I am only doing this because you always run away from me," Jake muttered against my hair.

I was taking my books out of the locker when Jake came up and hugged me from behind.

"Did you make a decision? Who will it be? Me or Aaron?" Jake's eyes bored into mine."

"Yes, and my decision is... NEITHER! You are both crazy so I'm not dating either of you," I said. "I'm gonna date that guy instead!" I pointed at a random guy by the water fountain.

"Carlos Ramirez?" Jake looked at me questioningly.

"Sure, yeah. Hey Carlos! Wait for me!" I squealed and ran after the poor unsuspecting teenager.

I went and grabbed his arm and gave him a big bright smile. You can't resist me now Carlos.

He gave me a pure confused look. "Errm...hi, who are you?" Carlos asked.

"Your new girlfriend, silly. You are single right?" I asked cheerfully.

"Yeah, but...."

"PERFECT! That means you are free. So let's go out from now, okay Papi?" I said seductively.

25. CHASING VIRGINS

Carlos was still in shock and was about to respond but Jake came behind him and grabbed his shoulder.

"Uhh...Jake?" Carlos said. His voice trembled as Jake gave him a death glare.

"Separate your arm from Janey and walk away," Jake ordered.

"Wha...what's going on? I am so confused..." said poor Carlos.

"SCRAM!" Jake roared. Carlos didn't hesitate for one second and ran like the wind. What an awful boyfriend candidate.

"That wasn't very nice. You scared my new boyfriend away," I pouted.

"Jane, stop screwing around. You are mine," Jake laughed.

"Whatever, I'm going to class," I said and did just that.

After class, I was having lunch outside. Then all of a sudden I noticed a girl with short blonde hair and cute round face. It was none other than Emily Johnson.

THE VIRGIN! I screamed inside my head. The one Mayra told me about. Jake's latest victim. I must go talk to her.

Emily looked at me.

"Hi, Emily!" I chirped.

She looked at me with confusion. "Hi..um..."

"It's Jane. You don't know me, no-one does," I said quickly.

"Oh hi. What's up?" she asked.

I decided to go straight to the point. "I wanted to talk to you about Jake Morris."

A shadow loomed over her face. She is probably having a war flashback from Jake's savagery.

"What about him?" she asked.

"I heard a rumor that...he took your virginity and ditched you. Is that true?" I asked. "I'm only asking because he is after me now," I added.

"It's kind of true but it's not what you think," Emily looked down.

I was curious now. "So what happened?" I asked.

"He didn't know I was a virgin. I always had a crush on him and it was me who went after him, not the other way around," she sighed.

I nodded and encouraged her to go on.

"Well, I told him I wanted to sleep with him. He asked me several times if

I was sure and if it was my first time. He told me he didn't want to do it if I was a virgin because he didn't want anything serious. But I liked him so much that I lied and told him I've done it many times before. He didn't realize until he...put it inside me..." she closed her eyes.

"Then what happened?" I urged her.

"He was mad at me first, then he acted all worried that he hurt me too much so I apologized to him for lying and we were okay. But things got kind of awkward between us at school so eventually, we stopped talking," she said.

"So he did ditch you!" I exclaimed.

"No no, it wasn't like that. He asked me out after we slept together but I said no," she said.

My eyes were wide with surprise. "Why? I thought you liked him?" I asked.

"Yes, but he didn't. I could tell by how guilty he looked and how distant he was from me," Emily said sadly.

"Then why do people think he is at fault?" I asked.

"He told me not to tell anyone. He said to play the victim if someone asks. He wanted to keep his bad boy reputation and I didn't want to look like a Slut so we mutually agreed to lie," she said.

"Why did you tell me the truth?" I asked.

Emily smiled. "I saw him hanging around you, teasing you in the hallways. Jake doesn't waste his time on girls he doesn't like. He is really into you Jane," she said.

I thanked her for telling the truth and walked away. What kind of person pretends to be an asshole and wants to look like a jerk. He is such a dimwit and it made me smile.

27

26. Making a Move

No, I wasn't going to date two guys at the same time. That's not who I am. I hardly wanted one relationship! I met both of them by accident and now they both want me. What kind of twilight zone bullshit is this!

But one thing for sure. Getting so much attention from them sure boosted my confidence! Aaron complimented me all the time. Him calling me beautiful made me think I've been hard on myself for all these years. Maybe I wasn't ugly after all.

And Jake...well, he wouldn't be caught dead complimenting me directly but once in a while he'd slip and say something sweet, but then try to cover it up with his endless teasing. Freaking idiot.

"What is this I hear about you dating both Aaron and Jake Morris?" Liliana asked me one day.

"I'm not dating them both. It's absurd," I denied.

"The rumor is circulating all around the school. I don't even have one boyfriend and you get to have two? That's just not fair!" she whined.

"Well dear sis, you are too picky with guys. So it's your fault for not having a boyfriend. You had your chance with Jake and you blew it," I said.

"He didn't really like me that much. He just liked my looks. As soon as we got to know each other he lost interest in me," Liliana waved her hands in frustration.

That's because you acted like you are too good for him and obsessed over Aaron, I thought.

I almost dropped my bowl of cereal as I heard someone honk their horn right outside my house.

What now? I thought and ran over to the window.

Jake was standing outside, leaning over a Mustang GT convertible and obnoxiously honking the horn. Because of course, why wouldn't he?

I was so startled I ran outside without my shoes on.

"What the hell?" I asked.

"Look, Janey! I got a new car," he said and waved his hand in front of it like an advertising model.

"Yes, I can see that. Congratulations, but why are you in front of my house so early in the morning?" I asked.

"So I can take you for a ride, duh, hop in," he smirked.

"Um...no thanks, I'm going inside now, bye," I said and tried to leave but he grabbed my wrist.

"You are coming with me sweet thang and it's final," he stared at me intently.

"Ugh...fine, let me go change," I said.

"No need, you look fine. Let's go," he said and pulled me toward his car. I'm being kidnapped!

I was wearing a loose t-shirt paired with some leggings. My hair was piled up on top in a messy bun. I looked like a mess.

"But Jake...I am not wearing any shoes!" I protested.

"You don't need them," he chuckled and picked me up bridal style then carried me to the car.

"Something is wrong with you boy," I yelled. I saw my neighbor Mrs. Higgins staring at us from across the street. Oh good, she'll save me. I looked at her helplessly.

"Good morning Jane! I see you found yourself a handsome fella, good for you!" she shouted.

Well, what the heck Mrs. Higgins...

He drove like he was being chased by a tornado. I wish I was wearing

26. MAKING A MOVE

something cute on the day I am about to die. He went inside a parking deck in a tall building.

"Where are we?" I asked.

"Just wait and see," he said mysteriously.

He parked on the roof and got out then picked me up and put me down on the hood of the car.

"Wow, you can see the whole city from up here!" I exclaimed.

"Yup, my dad owns this building so I'm allowed to access the roof," he said.

"Why did you bring me here?" I asked.

He didn't say anything and took something out of his car then held it in front of my face.

A chocolate cupcake?

"Is that for me..." I asked but before I could say more he practically shoved it inside my mouth.

I was going to curse him out but stopped as I started to chew it. It was amazing. Can't get mad at something so sweet and delicious!

"It's good right?" he smiled.

"Mmhmm," I nodded. "What's it for?" I asked.

"It's my birthday," he said.

"Oh? Happy Birthday!" I said cheerfully.

He gave me another warm smile but his eyes turned sad all of a sudden.

"Thanks, this is the gift from my parents," he said and pointed at the car.

"Wow, you are so lucky. My parents gave me a pair of socks and a used video game last year. I do like the game though don't get me wrong," I said. He didn't say anything and looked at the view.

"How come you aren't spending it with your parents and Aaron?" I asked.

"Aaron went on a college tour. He sent me a nice birthday message though," he said.

"And your parents?" I asked.

"They handed me the keys to this and took off to London for vacation. It's just a birthday. I guess it's not as important to them," Jake said bitterly.

I felt really bad all of a sudden. He was lonely. Come to think of it, their parents were never home even though they are just teenagers. At least Aaron was out of school and can take care of himself, but Jake was still young.

"You should've told me earlier. I could've gotten you a present," I said.

"You still can," his eyes were twinkling with mischief.

"I can?" I could already tell the answer is not going to be good.

"Yes," he leaned over to me. "How about a birthday blowjob?" he whispered.

"EWW! No way you freak! In your dreams," I laughed and punched him on the chest.

"Ouch! You hurt my heart, Janey. On my birthday too," he pouted.

"Jerk," I said.

"How about a kiss then?" he asked.

I suppose a kiss wouldn't hurt since we've done a couple of times anyway.

I gently pressed my lips on his. He cupped my cheeks and pulled me closer, deepening the kiss. He pressed me down on the hood of the car, his hands started to wander around my body.

I should tell him to stop, I thought. I felt his warm fingers under my shirt, his hand was dangerously close to my breasts. My mind was starting to get clouded. I can't think straight when he touched me like this.

"Mmm...Jake, you should stop..." I moaned against his mouth as he kept sucking on my lips and my tongue.

I jolted as he slid his hand inside my leggings. That's when my defense mechanism kicked in and I kneed him between his legs.

28

27. The Birthday Boy

"OW! Son of a motherfucking asshole!" Jake screamed and laid down on the back seat. He held his crotch and groaned in pain.

"That's what you get for getting all rapey on me, you idiot," I said.

"Ugh Janey...it hurts," he whined.

I felt kind of bad. Maybe I kneed him harder than I intended. I ran over to him and looked down.

"Are you okay? Did I break your balls?" I said with fake concern.

"I don't know, take a look," he said and pulled me down on top of him then flipped me over. He tricked me!

"Get off of me, you imbecile," I struggled underneath him.

"Not until you apologize," he laughed.

"No way, you should've kept your hands to yourself," I whined.

His eyes softened. "Yeah, sorry. I got carried away. I'd never force myself on you, I promise," he said.

Jake? Apologizing? That's a first.

"I'm sorry too. I didn't mean to hit you that hard," I said.

"I think I'm okay. We can still make a bunch of babies together don't worry," Jake grinned dubiously.

"Hah, you wish," I said but I could already feel myself blushing. Why did he have to go and say stuff like this to me?

"Thank you for spending time with me on my birthday," he said. His eyes were dark again.

I remembered what Emily told me. About him liking me. The way he was acting was making me believe his feelings were real. But what about me, do I like him? All I knew was my heart fluttered uncontrollably every time he was near me.

"I...I want to spend the whole day with you. If...you want?" I said nervously.

Jake's eyes lit up. "Really? You mean it?" he asked.

"Yeah, it's your birthday so...I don't want you to be alone. But that is if you promise not to harass me," I said

"I'll try not to," he chuckled.

"But first, I need to go home and change. I look like a hobo," I said.

"Whatever you say. I still think you are fine but I'll take you home," he said.

I changed while he waited for me in the living room. I put on a cute shirt and paired it with white shorts. My hair was having one of its wild days so there was nothing I could do with it in such a short amount of time so I just left it alone.

"Where to now, good sir?" I asked him.

"My house, so I can get you alone and do innapropriate things to you," he said casually.

"Nevermind then, have fun spending your birthday alone," I said.

"I am joking! Jeez, we are just going to play some video games or something. You like that right?" he asked.

"Okay," I said quietly. I would be lying if I said the thought of spending alone time with him didn't make me nervous. But I promised to spend the whole day with him so a promise is a promise, right?

I spent the day playing video games and bickering with Jake. Surprisingly enough, he didn't try to make a move on me the entire time. Maybe my knee to his crotch taught him a lesson.

He is actually fun to hangout with when he is not being a jerk. He was funny and kind of adorable.

Did I just call Jake Morris adorable? I must've gone insane already.

27. THE BIRTHDAY BOY

"What do you want to do now?" he asked.

"Let's bake a cake," I said.

"You know how to bake?" he raised his eyebrows.

"Yup, one of my specialty. Then after I finish baking it, we are going to sit in front of the window together like in the movie, sixteen candles," I announced.

"You are such a dork," Jake rolled his eyes but he was smiling. "I'm not even turning sixteen. I turned seventeen."

"Huh? You were my age till now? But you are a senior," I was confused. He was kind of young to be a senior.

Jake seemed uncomfortable. "Yeah...I kind of skipped a grade."

"YOU!? Skipped a grade? Hahaha..." I chuckled. "Oh, you are serious."

He shrugged.

"Wait..that means you are smart. Then why did you make me come over that day to help you with math?" I asked.

"I don't want anyone to know I'm a straight A student. I have to keep up with my hooligan reputation. And...I asked you because I just wanted an excuse to hangout with you," he gave me a shy smile.

Who is this guy and what did he do with the bad boy Jake?

"And you said I was a nerd," I grinned.

"You better not tell anyone or I'll make you pay Jane Brown!" he threatened me.

"Whatever, let's get baking," I said and dragged him into the kitchen.

It took me an hour to get that cake in the oven even though it should've taken me no more than 30 minutes because Jake won't stop messing around.

"Thank you so much for dumping an entire bowl of flour on my head and screaming *Janey your hair turned grey*, you stupid shit," I said angrily.

"It was an accident," Jake said nonchalantly.

"A-ha...sure. I need to borrow your shower and clothes," I said and looked at my shirt which was covered in flour and sticky frosting.

Jake took out a t shirt and threw it at me. "You can borrow this," he said.

I immediately went to take a shower and wash my hair. Why is it every time I hang out with Jake, my night ends in chaos?

Ah much better, I thought as I stepped out of the shower.

Jake was sitting by the window, waiting for me.

"Hey, I'm done," I said quietly.

He looked at me but didn't say anything and just stared at me.

"Wha...what?" I asked. I was suddenly feeling nervous as his heated eyes trailed up and down on my body.

"I like you in my shirt," he said. His voice gotten lower and huskier somehow.

He stepped closer and grazed his fingers on my cheek, sending a jolt of electricity through my veins. I hated the fact that he affected me this much.

"I want to touch you more. Is that okay?" he whispered.

I gulped. His fingers on my skin was making me hot. My mind was telling me I should say no but my body wanted more of his touch. I was doomed from the start as there is no way I could resist him.

29

28. Making Me His

"J...Jake w...wait," I tried to protest but my voice was barely audible as he leaned down and kissed my neck. I put my hands on his chest, intending to push him away but I just left them there.

He covered my face and neck with small kisses.

"You want me to stop? Just say the words and push me away," he growled and put his arms around my waist. His eyes were boring into my soul.

"I just...I hate you!" I declared and pressed my lips on his. I closed my eyes as our mouth moved in perfect sync. I could feel his hands tightening on my waist. As our body pressed against each other, I felt his erection, but this time, it didn't freak me out.

"Janey," he whispered and stared into my eyes. He didn't say anything else but he didn't have to. I knew he wanted me from the way he was looking at me with those heated eyes.

I couldn't control myself anymore. I slipped my tongue inside his mouth and kissed him hungrily. I wrapped my legs around his waist as he grabbed my hips to pick me up in his arms.

"You are so beautiful, Jane," he hovered over me and said.

What? I never thought I'd hear *that* come out of his mouth.

"You are just saying that because I practically threw myself at you," I giggled. Shoot, here come my insecurities, popping up when it's not wanted.

"Janey, don't start with me. You are fucking beautiful and sexy," Jake insisted.

"But people sa-..." I started to protest but Jake crushed his lips on my lips and sealed them shut with a kiss.

"I don't care what people say, I know what I'm looking at," he said after breaking the kiss.

I blushed. I couldn't say anything else as I looked into his brown eyes that were dark with desire for me. He meant it when he said he wanted me.

But was I ready to give myself to him? At this point, we weren't even in a relationship. What if he doesn't want anything to do with me after this? What if I was just here for his mere pleasure? What if...

He took his shirt off and all of my doubts vanished because sweet baby Jesus, look at those abs!

Listen, I know I sound like a total shallow Slut, but my whole life I was ignored as the ugly, plain Jane. So excuuse me for wanting to treat myself with this perfect specimen in front of me. I deserve it.

He slid his hand inside my shirt and touched my breasts. I shivered. He lifted up my shirt and placed soft kisses all over my body.

"Don't kick me this time, okay? I promise I won't do anything you don't want me to," he said quietly.

I giggled. "I'm sorry about that, please don't stop," I groaned.

He smirked and grazed his finger on my lips. "I fucking love these pouty lips," he said in a hoarse whisper.

I wish he'd stop saying things like that because I could feel myself slowly losing control.

He took my shirt off completely. "Damn... your body feels like its burning. You want me that much, huh," he grinned and took off my underwear. I've never felt so exposed but for once I didn't care.

He licked his finger then slipped it in and out of me, emitting soft moans from within my throat.

"You are nice and tight, just the way I like it," he whispered in my ears and nibbled on my neck.

"Tha...that's b..because it's my first time, stupid," I whimpered as he put two more fingers in.

28. MAKING ME HIS

"Normally, I wouldn't go this far if it's a girl's first time, but you are special. You are my Janey and I want all of you!" his voice sounded thick with emotions and lust.

Jake, you whore..

He took out his penis and I instinctively gasped. This is it, I was about to lose my virginity.

"I'll give you one last chance Jane, are you sure you want this? Because once it's done you'll be all mine," he asked gently as he put on the condom.

"Ugh. I want you and you are driving me crazy by delaying the process," I cried. Just do me already goddammit. I wanted him to ravage me and make a mess of me.

He didn't ask questions anymore and pushed inside me. He stopped as I moaned in pain. "I'll go slow," he whispered and kissed my mouth. The pain was soon replaced by pleasure as he moved slowly on top of me.

"Is this okay? Am I hurting you?" he asked and continued to kiss my face and neck while he thrust in and out of me.

"I'm okay, you can move faster," I said in between small gasps. He gazed into my eyes then all of a sudden his movement became faster and deeper.

A bubble burst insider and I climaxed, screaming his name. He couldn't hold it anymore and came, then collapsed on top of me.

30

29. Bringing Back the 80s

"Are you going to get off of me? You weigh a ton!" I cried as Jake was still lying on top of me.

"Yup, all muscle weight and not an ounce of fat baby," he bragged.

I rolled my eyes.

"Hey did you mean what you said earlier? When you said I was beautiful?" I asked. I couldn't help it. It was still hard for me to trust a compliment. Especially when it was coming from Jake.

"I'm not the kinda guy to flatter girls so I can get them into bed Janey. I meant what I said. You still doubt me?" he was concerned.

"It's just that, in the past, you said the same thing as everyone. You said I was plain. You were into Liliana more than me because she is beautiful as everyone says," I pouted. I wasn't going to let him off easily. He made me feel so bad and ugly at times!

"I said a lot of stupid shit I didn't mean. Honestly, I wasn't into her as much as you think. Ever since the day you fell on top of me, I kept wanting to know you. I used Liliana as an excuse to get close to you. I was a stupid kid who had no idea how to talk to someone so smart and beautiful. Because girls usually approached me first. And you never even looked in my direction," Jake exhaled.

What! Was I dreaming about this conversation? Or did Jake hit his head and lost his mind?

29. BRINGING BACK THE 80S

"I don't get it. Why are you like this?" I gasped.

"Fuck if I know," he chuckled.

I got up to get dressed. I can't believe I had sex with Jake Morris. I need a lot of time to process the whole situation. My eyes widened as I remembered something important.

"What is it?" Jake asked curiously.

"Oh my God! MY CAKE!" I screamed and ran to the kitchen. I prayed it didn't burn.

But thankfully it was okay. I can have my sixteen candles moment with Jake.

"Is it okay? Did our baby survive?" Jake poked his head inside the kitchen.

"Yes, phew. I wasn't too late," I sighed. The cake looked perfect. Somehow it wasn't burnt to a crisp. I took it out of the oven and spread some frosting on it then decorated with some candles.

Jake and I sat in front of the window with the cake. Yes, I made him do it. Just like in sixteen candle. He was my Molly Ringwald.

"This is stupid. I'm not a sixteen-year-old girl and this isn't a corny 80s movies," Jake said irritably.

"Shh...you are ruining the moment. Just blow out the candle and make a wish," I said. He did as he was told. I like the compliant Jake he was far cuter than the bully Jake.

"So...who's gonna tell Aaron?" he asked, suddenly turning serious.

Shit Aaron...I need to break things off with Aaron. He would be so mad when he finds out I slept with his brother!

"I think you should tell him since he is your brother," I suggested.

"No, I think you should tell him since *you* got together with him in the beginning," Jake said.

"Well, it was *your* fault that he saw me so *you* should tell him," I countered.

We argued back and forth for another 5 minutes but couldn't agree on anything.

"Anyway, I should go home, it's getting late," I said.

"Okay," he looked so sad for a second that I had the urge to grab him and kiss his face but I controlled myself.

He dropped me off at home. "Ah...I'll see you at school tomorrow then?" he said awkwardly.

"Y...yeah...tomorrow," I said. I wondered if I'll ever look at him the same again.

"Wait...Jane," I stopped as he called me. "Yeah?" I said.

"I didn't sleep with you just because you were a virgin. I don't have a thing for virgins, just so you know. I really like you," he said.

I smiled. "I know. I really like you too."

"And now that our first time is out of the way, you get to become my sex slave," he smirked.

"Never mind! I don't like you anymore!" I cried and ran off while he laughed behind me. Imbecile.

31

30. Being Kidnapped

I thought I'd regret what happened the next day but I feel great. I don't even care if he turns back into a jerk because I wasn't scared of him anymore. Jake wasn't exactly the intimidating asshole he made himself out to be. He was actually kind of sweet. He can pretend all he wants but I'm not letting it bother me anymore.

All I can think now is I miss him. It has been only a day since I last saw him and I already can't wait to see him. What if he pretends not to know me when I see him at school though? I'd be really hurt.

All my doubts vanished when I came out of the house in the morning because there he was, in all his glory, standing right outside my house with his shiny new car.

"JAKE!" I screamed and threw myself at him. I don't even care that I look like a clingy bitch.

He laughed and took me in his arms then kissed me.

"My dick was that good, Huh?" he remarked.

"Shut up, that's not why. I thought you'll pretend not to know me after we were done," I said awkwardly.

"You have some serious self-esteem issues, Janey. Or is that what you secretly want? You want me to go back to being a jerk to you? Does that make you hot my little masochist?" he grinned.

"Ugh...no thanks. What are you doing here?" I asked.

"I am here to take my wifu to school, what else," he said.

"If you are going to give me more cringy nicknames then I prefer you go back to being the asshole Jake," I looked at him in shock.

"Too late wifu. You are my girl now," he laughed.

I couldn't say anything else anymore and looked at him with admiration. It's like he gets even more handsome when he laughs.

We didn't have any classes together at school so I didn't see him until lunch. I saw him sitting in the cafeteria. Three girls flocked around him like a moth to a flame.

Oh hell no. His man whorish ways end today.

I stood in front of them and cleared my throat.

"Can we help you?" one of the fangirls asked.

"I need to talk to Jake. Alone," I said.

"Who the hell are you?" The other girl barked.

Jake stood up and put his arms around me. "Sorry girls, wifu needs alone time so get out of here. Thanks for stopping by," he smirked.

The girls had a horrified look on their face. And so did I. My face turned beet red. Did he really have to say crazy stuff like this all the time?

"You know you are not helping me. Now I have more girls hating me, like dealing with Mayra wasn't bad enough?" I frowned.

"Let them come at my girlfriend and see what happens!" he said seriously.

"Girlfriend?" I could hardly contain my excitement.

"What, you think you can have sex with me and then act as nothing happened? I told you you are mine from now on," Jake said quietly.

Is this really happening? Am I allowed to be this happy?

I got a text from Aaron later that day. My happiness turned into guilt. I didn't know how to tell him about Jake and me. I've never broke things off with someone before since I never had a boyfriend. I decided to meet up with him and tell him in person.

And I wasn't going to do this alone. I'm taking Jake down with me.

"What if he beats me up?" Jake said.

"Why would he do that, he is your brother," I rolled my eyes. "Besides, I

30. BEING KIDNAPPED

thought you said it was up to me to decide who I want to be with."

"Yeah but Aaron is a bit...temperamental. Once he is into someone or something, he doesn't like to give them up easily. He also has abandonment issues," Jake said.

Fuck...why is he just telling me this now.

"Either way, I'm telling him and you are coming with me," I said.

"Alright fine, I'll come with you. But if he beats me up and cripples me, you are responsible for taking care of me for the rest of my life. That includes helping me wipe my ass," Jake declared.

"There's something seriously wrong with you Jake," I shook my head.

I went to their house in the afternoon to talk.

"Hey, Jane, what brings you here? Not that I am complaining," he said.

"I...um...we... JAKE! It's your turn!" I squealed and pushed Jake forward.

"The fuck...you didn't even say anything," Jake complained.

"What is going on?" Aaron demanded to know.

"I decided I like Jake," I said quietly. "I wasn't sure at first, but the attraction between us is too strong to ignore," I added.

Aaron didn't say anything at first and stared at me intently. He cleared his throat. "I see...what about you Jake? How do you feel about Jane?"

"I really like her too," he said.

"Well, I don't accept!" Aaron cried, startling both of us. "You are just confused, Jane! This whole time you've been saying you don't like him but now all of a sudden, you do? And Jake, you've never wanted to be with a girl other than wanting to have sex with her."

"Jane is different," Jake protested.

"Aaron I'm sorry. We aren't trying to hurt you," I said.

"You belong with me, Jane," Aaron said. He was starting to scare me now.

"I can't be with you Aaron, Jake and I..." before I could finish my sentence, Jake pulled me away from him.

"You can't tell him we had sex," he whispered. "He is hot-headed, we don't know what he might do."

"What are you two whispering about over there?" Aaron roared.

This was not how I imagined it to go down.

"I'm going to give you another chance to think about this because I'm not losing to my little brother," Aaron said.

"This isn't a competition," Jake protested.

"Meanwhile, you are coming with me," Aaron said and grabbed my hand then started to drag me away with him.

"Aaron! Let go. Jake!" I cried.

"Wait! Aaron, don't hurt her!" Jake yelled behind us.

Aaron pushed me inside his car. "We are going for a ride," he said. I could hear the rage in his voice that shook me to my core.

Why didn't you try harder to help me Jake, ya dummy, I thought.

32

31. Waifu...What?

I opened my mouth to say something but closed it back up when I looked at Aaron. He looked angry. Beyond furious. I'm being kidnapped by the angry former bad boy so I am screwed beyond epic proportions.

He finally stopped the car somewhere and exhaled. Maybe he is calm enough to hear me out. I wanted to explain to him that what happened between Jake and I are a mere accident. I didn't mean to ditch him for Jake.

"He fucked you didn't he?" was the first thing he said.

I cringed. "That's an ugly way of putting it but yes, we had sex. It was consensual. I really like him Aaron," I said quietly.

"But why? What does he have that I don't have?" Aaron looked at me.

"Um...I didn't like him at first because I thought he was just a douche bag but he turned out to be a lot different than I imagined. He can be really sweet when he wants to be," I said. I will admit it was typical of me to fall for the bad boy but Jake was kind of special.

"But I was good to you from the beginning! He was a jerk to you!" Aaron cried.

"I know and I appreciate it. You are an amazing guy, Aaron, but you are not the guy for me. When I kissed him, everything changed. It was nothing like I've ever felt before," I said.

"You are just confused. Maybe I should remind you," Aaron said and pressed his lips on mine and kissed me forcefully. This time his kiss didn't feel nice, it felt wrong in every way possible. Because he wasn't Jake.

The car door opened all of a sudden and someone pulled me out.

"Jake! You are here? How did you find us?" I was surprised.

"I followed you. You think I'd let my girlfriend get kidnapped by my brother?" Jake said and held me tightly against him. His heart was beating really fast. I wondered if he saw Aaron kissing me and got jealous. I wouldn't blame him.

"Girlfriend?" Aaron sounded amused.

"Yes. And eventually, she'll be my waifu and we'll have five children. Two boys and three girls," Jake smirked.

What the...what? Only Jake would come up with a ridiculous scenario like that. I rolled my eyes.

"Okay, no. I didn't agree to the second part," I told Aaron. Both of these brothers are clinically insane.

"You said you didn't like her and called her plain Jane!" Aaron accused.

"That's because I was stupid and blind. She is beautiful. I mean look at her crazy and wild hair, so cute. And these big beautiful eyes," Jake looked at me fondly.

Aww Jakey... I thought.

"And these cute little chubby cheeks, they are so squishy," Jake pinched my cheeks.

"Ouch! You jerk. They aren't chubby. It's just water weight," I whined. I don't like him anymore. Take me back Aaron!

"And I love the cute noises she makes when I put my di-..." I slapped my hand on his mouth before he could finish. I'm going to kill him later.

Aaron got out of the car and slammed the door shut. "You know what, fine. If that's what you both want then so be it. But don't come crying to me, when he breaks your heart, Jane," he said and glared at us with those intense green eyes. He got back inside his car and drove off.

"Is he going to be okay?" I asked Jake.

"Don't worry, he'll come around," he reassured me.

I didn't want to hurt him as he was the first person to be so sweet and caring

31. WAIFU...WHAT?

to me. But my heart wanted Jake and I couldn't ignore it.

33

32. Jake's Fan Club

It has been a week since Jake and I started going out. People at school were whispering about us since it was unlikely for Jake to have a girlfriend. Especially, when the girlfriend is someone like me. Not some hot blonde with a rocking body.

I was cornered by the same two girls after school that was flirting with Jake the other day. Seriously, I get the appeal but why attack me instead of Jake? Besides, he can't be the only cute guy in school.

"Oh, you must be from the Jake Morris fan club," I smirked.

"The what?" one of the girls asked. She looked confused.

"I don't get it. Why is Jake so crazy about you? You are just some goody two shoes. And you aren't even that pretty!" the blonde one said. Ouch, harsh.

"Oh em gee, I know right!" I squealed sarcastically. "You should go ask him though," I suggested.

"I bet you let him get inside your pants. Slut!" the brunette said.

It only happened once, jeez.

"Let's fuck her up," the blonde said. Jesus...what kind of school is this.

"Ladies please, there must be more guys here other than Jake! Give them a chance!" I exclaimed.

"I've been trying to get with him since sophomore year. But he got together with Mayra instead. I heard she is out of the picture now and you just waltz in out of nowhere and take him away from me? It's not fair!" the blonde whined.

32. JAKE'S FAN CLUB

So Jake is a playboy after all. I'm going to have to scold him later.

"Look I'm sorry but I like Jake. Even if you beat me up I'm not going to leave him so you and your girlfriend can take a hike," I glared at them. He was mine now bitches.

"What's going on here?" All three of us turned around.

Jake was standing right there giving me the puppy dog eyes.

"Your fan club is trying to fight me?" I laughed nervously.

"My fan club?" Jake was confused.

"We weren't doing anything to her," the brunette said quickly. "Let's go, Shelley," she said and tugged at the blonde.

"No, let's settle this. Once and for all," Shelley declared. "Jake, you can't ignore me forever. You promised if you stopped seeing Mayra we would be together!" she said.

"I didn't promise you anything Shelley," Jake looked frustrated. I wasn't serious about anyone before. But I'm with Jane now," he placed his hand on the small of my back.

Shelley's face turned red and she started to walk away.

"Wait, Shelley!" she turned around as Jake called her.

"If you ever threaten my girlfriend again you'll have to deal with me," he said menacingly.

Fear reflected in Shelley and her friend's eyes and they quickly strode away.

"Seriously Jake, will this ever end? How many girls have you slept with?" I said irritably.

"Hmm...lets see...Emily, Mayra, Shelley, the cheerleading squad..." he started to count with his fingers.

"Eww! You probably have diseases. To think I let you inside me. I'm breaking up with you!" I cried and tried to get away from him but he grabbed me then started to drag me away.

He pushed me inside an empty classroom and locked the door.

"What are you doing?" I gasped.

"I slept with two other girls before you. Mayra and Emily," his eyes softened.

"But..I heard..." I hesitated.

"Who you going to believe, Janey? The gossipers or me?" he said and put my hand on his chest. "You feel that? My heart is going wild just from being near you. It didn't do it for them, not even when I slept with them," he said and grazed his lips on my cheeks.

I blushed. My heart was pounding too. It hurts to be close to him because my body craves him too much.

34

33. Dealing with Insecurities

Jake slid his hand inside my shirt and stroked my stomach and breasts, his lips never leaving mine. His hand felt warm and rough against my skin.

"Nn..no Jake, not here!" I said weakly. It felt so good. The last thing I wanted was for him to stop touching me but we were at school!

"You don't sound too convincing," he said and unzipped my skirt then slipped his fingers inside my underwear.

"JAKE!" I protested but a moan escaped from my throat. Pleasure jolted through my veins at the mere touch of his finger on my clit.

"Shh....keep your voice down or we might get in trouble," Jake whispered in my ear.

He moved his finger in and out. I'm ashamed to admit that despite my protests, I was soaking wet down there.

"Does this feel good?" Jake asked. His voice sounded so deep and gentle that it turned me on even more than before.

"Y..yes..but you are mean for doing this to me here," I whimpered.

He chuckled and cupped my cheek with his other hand then kissed me. I could feel my body heat rising as he quickened the movements of his fingers while his tongue urgently stroked the inside of my mouth. I wrapped my arms around his neck to keep myself steady as I felt my body losing control. My entire body trembled violently when I came.

He held me for a moment then slowly took his fingers out. "You okay?" he asked in an amused tone.

"No, I'm not okay, you asshole. I'm better than okay," I tried to breathe normally as my body was still recovering from the ecstasy.

He laughed. "I'm glad I could be of service," he pecked my cheek. "Let's get you home now."

"Huh? But what about you? Don't you want some too?" I said and pointed at his bulge.

"Awe you are too sweet to think of me, waifu. But I just wanted to do this for you. So you know how crazy I'm about you," Jake said. "Think of it as an apology on behalf of my *fan club*," he smirked.

"Oh, I forgive them," I said. Now I get what the fuss is about. Of course, they want him. He is an absolute gem. I am never letting him go, they are going to have to pry him out of my cold dead hands.

I fixed my clothes and let him drive me home.

"Would you want to come have dinner with me and my parents tomorrow night?" Jake asked.

"Sure..will Aaron be there too?" I asked hesitantly.

"Yes, but don't worry about him. It's going to be fine," Jake reassured me.

But I was worried. Not only do I have to face Aaron but I also will be meeting their parents for the first time. I am not just worried, I'm scared shitless.

On the night of the dinner, I borrowed a nice dress from Liliana. I really need to expand my wardrobe.

"So you and Jake are pretty serious now huh?" Liliana asked.

"Yeah, he is great," I said cheerfully. "I think I'm falling for him," I blushed.

"Just be careful," she said quietly.

"He isn't as bad as he acts. He cares about me," I protested.

"I'm not talking about him. I'm talking about the girls who used to hang around him. They hate you now. I bet they are plotting your murder as we speak," Liliana said.

"I can handle them. What do you care anyway?" I said pointedly.

"I know you think I hate you but you are my sister. I do care about you," she said.

33. DEALING WITH INSECURITIES

Well, that's a shocker. "Then why do you act like such a bitch to me?" I asked.

"I just...I'm sort of jealous of you. People may find me more beautiful but that's all I am. I'm not as smart as you are. My looks are all I have. And when Aaron showed more interest in you, my jealousy turned into hatred," she said.

"You are smart too Liliana," I said gently.

"I wish people would see there's more to me than my looks," she sounded frustrated.

I was surprised by her confession. I guess we both had to deal with our insecurities.

35

34. A New Face

I felt like it was all my fault for creating this messy situation. I shouldn't have gone out with Aaron to spite Liliana. He was an amazing guy and he deserved better. I hoped this situation wouldn't mess up the relationship between the two brothers.

"What are you thinking about?" Jake asked me. We were hanging out at Jake's front yard after school.

"Aaron," I said and sipped on my juice distractedly.

"You have the audacity to think about my brother when I am sitting right in front of you?" he remarked.

"It's not what you think," I said irritably. "I just feel so bad. He had been nothing but a sweetheart to me and look at what I did. I sighed.

Jake moved closer and kissed me on the cheek. "You did nothing wrong. He is just throwing a mini tantrum because I got the best girl." his eyes were sparkling.

I blushed. I couldn't be too mad at my decision. Jake is a cutie patootie.

"JAAAAKE!" I almost spit my juice out when I heard a shrill voice calling for him.

A cute redhead frantically waved her hands and ran towards us. Her long ponytail bounced as she frolicked. Her skirt almost riding up her butt because of the wind.

Jake's face changed from pleasant to sour in seconds. Great...is this another

34. A NEW FACE

member of Jake Morris fan club?

"Oh my god, Jake! I am so glad to see you!" she said and attacked him with a hug. Oh hell no, she is getting cooties all over my Jake!

"Um...yeah...hi Bella. What are you doing in this neighborhood?" Jake said. He looked uncomfortable. I gave him the 'we need to talk' look.

"YOU ARE NEVER GOING TO BELIEVE THIS!" she was shouting now. "I just moved in next door to you. Isn't that awesome?" she chirped excitedly.

"Ahem..." I cleared my throat to let her know I was sitting in front of her. Or else I felt like she would keep pretending I didn't exist.

"Sorry...um...this is my girlfriend Jane. Jane this is Bella, she was in the same class as Aaron," Jake introduced us.

"Awe how cute! I thought you'd never get a girlfriend but I am glad you met a cute girl," Bella winked at me.

Okay, I like this fangirl a whole lot.

"Anyways...where is Aaron?" she said. Her eyes were glinting.

"He is not home so you should come back some other day," Jake.

"Okay! Well bye, Jane and Jake. I'll be seeing a lot of you since I live right across the street. Bye!" she declared and bounced her way back to her house which really was right across the street.

I turned to Jake and gave him a quizzical look.

"What?" he asked innocently.

"What you mean *what*? Who is she?" I asked.

"That's Bella Davis, who is apparently my neighbor now," he smirked.

"Yes, I got that part, you nincompoop. What is your relationship with her? Is she part of your Jake fan club?" I was annoyed.

Jake laughed. "Hell no. She has no interest in me. She is actually part of Aaron's fan club," he said.

Something clicked in my brain. There is a girl who lives across the street who used to like Aaron?

"Oh my god, I know! We can set her up with Aaron!" I said.

Jake looked scared all of a sudden. He coughed nervously. "Yeah...that's not a good idea," he said.

I looked at him with surprise.

"I don't understand. Why not? She is pretty and seems very friendly," I asked.

"It's a long story," Jake tried to dismiss the subject but I won't let go that easily.

"I wanna know. Tell me everything!" I insisted.

Jake sighed. "Okay, Bella seems normal at first but she is actually a total nutcase," he said.

"That's not very nice," I gasped.

"No, you don't understand. She really is crazy. She had been after Aaron since his freshman year. She stalked him, left love letters in his locker, and even stole his jacket at one point. I am sure she has a shrine of Aaron in her bedroom," Jake chuckled.

"That's hilarious," I said.

Jake shook his head. "It was funny at first but she got really annoying. She told everyone they were going out. She would always found a way to chase all the girls off, you know...the ones who liked Aaron," he said.

"Wow...she is persistent," I remarked.

"I am sure Aaron will move out of this state once he hears about her moving back across the street," he smirked.

"Why did she move away?" I asked. This girl intrigues me.

"No one knows. I heard something about a death in the family," Jake said.

I thought about it for a second. "Maybe he should give her another chance. Maybe she is less psychotic now?" I offered.

"We will find out soon enough," Jake yawned. "Enough talking about the crazy Bella. How about you and me take this party upstairs?" he leaned in for a kiss but I pushed him away.

"How about no?" I said. As much as I love seeing Jake's hot body, I didn't want to jump into his bed every time he asked.

"Oh come on Janey, you know you want me," he whispered seductively. His warm breath tickled my neck and I shivered. Damn it...I do want him!

"Okay, but we are only going to make out a little bit, then I am leaving," I said.

He got up quickly and picked me up.

34. A NEW FACE

"Hey! What are you doing! You don't have to carry me, I can walk," I protested.

"Shh...just enjoy the princess treatment," he said so I didn't say anything else.

He pushed me down the bed and kissed me hungrily. His hands searched all over my body. He slipped his hands underneath my shirt. Excuse me...I thought we were just going to kiss!

"Mmm...Jake, don't...we can't do it right now," I whimpered. I tried to suppress my moans but they kept escaping. "What if Aaron or someone else comes home and sees us?"

"Aaron is at his friend's house and my parents are away for a business trip again. It's just you and me, baby," he lightly bit my lower lip and sucked on it. I couldn't deny how turned on I was. His hands all over my body were driving me wild.

"Janey, can we do it?" he looked at me with his eyes full of lust. I want to say yes so bad!

"No," I said and tried to keep a straight face. He must not know I want him just as bad!

"Please? I'll go real slow and make you feel so good," he said quietly and kissed my stomach.

I groaned. "Damn it! Fine, but this is the last time I'll let you pressure me into this," I said. My face was already beet red.

He grinned devilishly and proceeded to give me what he promised.

36

35. Dinner with Parents

On the night of the dinner with parents, I sat in front of Jake and Aaron's parents. The atmosphere was intimidating.

"So you are Jake's girlfriend? Jake never brought a girl before so this is a surprise," Jake's mom Tracy raised her eyebrows at me.

"That's because Jake acts like a fucking asshole all the time so he never had a real girlfriend," Aaron barked.

"Watch your language at the dinner table son," their father Michael commented.

"In case you forgot big bro, you weren't so angelic yourself," Jake said.

"At least I admit my faults. You are still an immature jerk who take things that didn't belong to him," Aaron's face was slowly turning red as he was getting angry.

"You don't get to tell me what's mine and what isn't," Jake said. His voice shook.

What the hell is going on? How did the conversation turn to this?

I could tell their parents were confused as well. Tracy looked at them with concern. "Everything okay with you two?" she asked.

"Everything is fine," Aaron muttered.

"Well, that's great then. Why don't you tell me about yourself, Jane?" Michael said. He already forgot about the confrontation at the table.

"Oh um...I go to school with Jake," I said nervously. I can still feel the

35. DINNER WITH PARENTS

hostility between Aaron and Jake. I felt bad for unintentionally causing it.

"Oh great. Frankly, I always imagined Jake to pick someone who is a bit more flashy or glamorous. I'm surprised he picked such a...girl next door," Tracy commented.

Ouch. Was that an insult? This isn't going well.

"Mom!" Jake glared at her.

"What? I'm just saying. Jane is cute and all but she is no beauty queen. Am I wrong?" Tracy shrugged.

Man, she is blunt. No wonder Jake and Aaron acts like a jerk.

"We don't have to listen to this. Let's go, Janey," he grabbed my hand and got up.

"Sit down, Jake," Michael ordered.

"Jake it's okay, I'm not offended or anything. Let's just eat," I let out a nervous chuckle and sat down, pulling him down with me.

"This dinner would've been much more pleasant if your bitch wife kept her mouth shut," Aaron said grimly.

"How dare you talk about me like that? Michael! Say something!" Tracy squealed.

"No need, I'm leaving," Aaron got up and stormed off.

What the hell is wrong with this family? I thought.

"I'm gonna go check on him," I said and got up. I felt somewhat responsible for things going south.

I found Aaron sitting outside on the porch.

"Hey, are you okay?" I asked.

"What do you care?" he said. His eyes were dark.

"I know you are still mad at me and Jake but you didn't have to snap at us. Especially at your mom!" I said.

"She is not my mom," Aaron. Said and looked away.

"Huh? She isn't?" I was curious.

"Nope. My mom died a long time ago. She is Jake's mom. We are half brothers," he said.

"Oh," I didn't know what to say.

"We've always been close but Jake always got everything he wanted because

Tracy spoiled him. I guess to make up for the fact that she was never there for him. I was the one who cared for him yet he still stole something I cared about. He stole you!" Aaron said angrily. His voice was filled with sadness.

I felt my heart twitch. I never realized how much I hurt him by choosing his brother over him. But I couldn't ignore my own heart.

"Aaron I'm sorry," I whispered.

He looked at me for a moment and pulled me toward him. Before I could stop him, he pressed his lips on mine and started to kiss me. I put my hands on his chest and was about to push him then I heard footsteps.

"Jane?"

My heart stopped as I heard Jake's voice behind me.

37

36. Misunderstanding

I pushed Aaron off but it was a little too late as Jake saw us kissing. I prayed that he didn't misunderstand me. All I wanted was to comfort Aaron because I felt bad for him.

"What the fuck are you doing bro?" Jake demanded to know.

"Claiming what should be mine," Aaron said.

"I'm not yours Aaron! Stop saying stuff like that!" I protested.

"Why would you let him kiss you, Janey?" Jake looked at me.

"I didn't! He kissed me. I was just talking to him and he…"

"You went too far Aaron," Jake turned to Aaron and scowled. "She is my girlfriend. She picked me! Just get over it already. Why can't you just be happy for me?" he said.

"Because I'm tired of looking out for you. My whole life I put your needs before mine. I got into fights with people in school. Only because you started shit with them and couldn't fight them by yourself! I took blames for you!" Aaron shouted.

I guess the rumors were all lies. Aaron wasn't a bully. He fought people to protect Jake.

"And just when I found the girl I like, you step in and steal her away. I'm done putting yourself before me," Aaron finished and exhaled.

"Wow, I didn't know you felt that way," Jake shook his head. "I'm sorry you had to do all that because I'm a fuck up, I really am. But it doesn't change the fact that Jane likes me."

"I don't care about your sorry. I'm not letting you have her. Before I thought I'd be okay if she chose either of us but I'm not okay with this at all," Aaron said and tried to grab me again. He had really gone crazy.

"Don't touch her!" Jake cried and charged at Aaron to interfere. Aaron instinctively swung his fist at him which landed directly on Jake's face.

I gasped loudly as I saw Jake crouching down holding his nose. Blood seeped through his fingers.

"Fuck...you broke my fucking nose," Jake groaned.

Aaron snapped out of his angry state when he saw Jake was hurt. The anger on his face was replaced by concern.

"Oh shit Jake, I didn't mean to hit you, buddy," Aaron ran over to him.

"Don't you fucking touch me, asshole! I can't believe you hate me this much! I thought you always had my back even though mom and dad don't give a shit about me. But I was wrong," he said. Sadness enveloped his face.

"Jake," I reached over to him.

"DON'T! This is all because of you. If we hadn't met you none of this would've happened," Jake said in a fit of anger and pain.

I jolted back in shock. His words were like a stab in my heart. I never meant to drive the two brothers apart. They both liked me at the same time. I never chose to be in this situation!

"I'm done with this," Jake stormed off holding his nose.

I just stood there, frozen in place.

"Uh...Jane," Aaron called me gently.

Tears started to stream down my cheeks. I couldn't control my emotions anymore. Is this it? Does Jake hate me now? But I didn't do anything wrong!

"I...I gotta go," I said and ran off sobbing.

I took an Uber home and cried all night. I couldn't believe how harsh he was. How is it my fault that Aaron is so hung up on me?

I faceplanted on the pillow. How could Jake say such mean things to me? He knows damn well it's not my fault that Aaron fought him over me. I get that he was hurt but he had no right to take it out on me!

36. MISUNDERSTANDING

That's it. I don't want to see either of them ever again.

I went to school the next day, mentally preparing myself to avoid Jake at all costs. I saw him in the halls. He had a bandage on his nose, the surrounding areas of his nose were black and blue. Aaron really got him good.

My instinct was to run over there and hug him until his pain goes away but my stupid stubborn self decided to pretend like I didn't care. But I did care. My heart hurts every time I looked at him.

He gave me a sad look when our eyes met but didn't say anything to me. I guess he was still mad at me? But why though? I didn't do anything!

The school was finally over and I got to go home. I couldn't wait to go home and drown in my own misery.

Aaron showed up at my front door a few hours later.

I was disappointed and mad at Aaron.

"Aaron you jerk! Just leave me alone! It's your fault my Jakey won't talk to me!" I cried, my eyes were already tearing up.

He sighed. "Look, I came here to apologize. I acted like a child and I forced myself on you. I'm sorry," he said.

"You can't force someone to be with you. I...I love Jake!" I said and sobbed incessantly.

"You love him?" He sounded surprised.

I paused as I realized what I just said. I confirmed my feelings for him without a second thought. I was in love with Jake Morris!

"Yes," I said quietly.

"Well good, then you should come take care of this idiot. He had been acting annoying since you left. Pretty sure I heard him cry at one point," Aaron sounded irritated.

"What are you talking about?" I was confused.

"He had been moping around because he yelled at you for no reason. Now he wants you back but he is too much of a coward to ask you directly to forgive him. Because he thinks you hate him. So please just come over and comfort him for fuck's sake. He is driving me crazy because it was my fault in the first place," Aaron said.

Jake doesn't hate me? My heart hammered against my chest.

"How do I know you aren't trying to trick me to kidnap me again?" I looked at him suspiciously.

"I really am sorry. I hope you believe me. I really liked you but I love my brother more. And I think he loves you too. He never acted like this over a girl before. He is a wreck and it has only been a day," Aaron said quietly.

"Did I hear Aaron's voice?" Liliana said from upstairs.

"Shit...we better get out of here," Aaron whispered. Fear reflected in his eyes and I couldn't help but giggle.

I quickly got into his car and he drove me to his house.

38

37. Mysterious Occurrence

I nervously knocked on his bedroom door. I hoped Aaron was telling me the truth and Jake wanted me back as much as I wanted him.

"GO AWAY AARON! I said I don't wanna come out," Jake and from inside.

"It..its Jane," I said.

The door flew open.

"Janey!" he cried and threw his arms around me and pulled me into a hug. I buried my face in his chest.

"I thought you would never speak to me again after the way I treated you. I'm so sorry," he whispered into my hair.

"I'm sorry too. For everything," I said. My eyes were full of tears. It felt too good to be in his arms.

"It wasn't your fault Janey. I was a jerk to you and my brother was the biggest idiot on the planet," he reassured me.

"*I deserve that!*" Aaron shouted from another room.

I tiptoed and smashed my lips against his.

"Ouch!" he cried. Shit, I forgot his nose was messed up.

"I'm so sorry!" I yelled.

Jake laughed. I stared at him with admiration. Even with his injuries, he was still beautiful.

"I heard you cried," I smirked.

Jake's expression turned serious. "Men don't cry. So that's bullshit information."

I giggled. "Well, I did. I thought I lost you," I said.

"I love you, Janey," he said and stared at me intently.

"Y...you do?" my voice shook. I didn't realize he felt the same way about me.

"Yes, let's never fight again, okay?" he said gently.

"I love you too!" I screamed. He pressed his lips on mine and kissed me, ignoring his pain. He grabbed my hips and pulled me closer to deepen the kiss.

"Are you two done being cringy? I have to go to the bathroom and you are blocking the way," Aaron said.

"Shut it Aaron, wifu and I trying to have a moment," Jake sneered.

Aaron rolled his eyes and kept walking but he was smiling. I guess he was serious when he said he got over me and Jake dating. At least, I hope so.

Jake wiped my tears away. "Now that we are back together, how about that make up sex?" he smirked.

"JAKE! Is that all you can think about?" I pouted.

He chuckled. "I am just joking. Unless you want me to..."

"NO!" I laughed and pushed him off.

I've never been so happy in my life. Besides the day I found Frederick's donuts but that was a different type of happiness. This time it was because I was in love.

"Hello! Jane? I was asking you a question," Liliana's annoying voice brought me back to reality.

"I love Jake," I said blissfully. I have no idea what question she asked me.

"Yes, I get it. We all do and it's annoying but I want you to tell me if you are all packed to go to grandma's house this weekend?" Liliana asked.

Oh. My whole family visits grandma in Connecticut at least twice a year. So I guess I was expected to go to. But that would mean I'll be out of state for a week. That also means I don't get to see Jake for two whole weeks!

"I don't wanna go," I declared.

37. MYSTERIOUS OCCURRENCE

"What's going on?" My mom walked in and asked.

"Jane says she doesn't wanna go to grandma's house," Liliana replied.

"We as a family have to go see her so you are going," my mom said irritably.

Ugh! No!

"What's the issue here?" my mom squinted her eyes at me.

"If she goes she wouldn't be able to see her precious boyfriend," Liliana rolled her eyes.

"Oh, that's what this is about?" mom asked.

"I finally get a boyfriend and you want to separate me from him for two weeks!" I pouted. I know I was being clingy and dramatic but I don't care.

My mom sighed. "Why don't you invite him to come with us then?" she suggested.

I brightened up. "Really? I can do that?" I asked.

"As long as you two behave, I don't see a problem," mom said.

Yes! Things were finally going my way. I get to be with Jake for two weeks! True, my family will be there too but still! This is going to be the best vacation ever!

I called Jake to give him the good news so he has enough time to ask his parents for permission.

Luckily, his parents aren't strict so they agreed right away.

Later in the week, the most unexpected thing happened. Aaron got a new girlfriend he met in college!

Okay, it's not THAT unexpected. Of course, as a handsome young guy, it's natural for him to find someone else in a short period of time. I only saw her a few times. Her name is Macie and she had a head full of pretty black hair, full lips, and a great body.

But before you think everything is perfect, let me tell you something. Things turned weird all of a sudden.

It all started when Macie came over one afternoon. Jake and I were hanging out in his room, making out like the horny teenagers we are. You know, the usual.

BANG!

An earth-shattering explosive noise rippled through the air and scared the bejesus out of me. I bit Jake's lips in the process.

"Ouch! You bit me!" Jake cried out and touched his lower lip.

"Oh my God, I'm so sorry! That noise scared me," I said.

"Yeah...what the hell is that about?" Jake said and proceeded to check it out.

Aaron ran out of his room at the same time, followed by Macie. She had a terrified expression on her face.

"What happened?" I looked at them curiously.

"Someone threw a rock at my window and broke it," Aaron said grimly and asked us the rock.

"Holy shit, that's huge! Who would do such a thing?" Jake asked.

"I'm guessing whoever wrote this note," Aaron said and handed us a piece of paper.

Break up with Macie or there will be a problem bigger than this rock, the note said.

39

38. Interview with a Stalker

"Who would do this!" Macie cried.

"I have an idea," I said.

Jake looked at me with surprise. "You do?"

"Well... it's just a theory but, didn't you say that girl across the street used to stalk Aaron?" I asked.

"What girl?" Aaron was confused. I guess he didn't run into his new neighbor yet.

"Wait, did you not notice Bella Davis moving in front of us?" Jake smirked. "Sorry, I forgot to tell you."

Aaron's eyes went wide as he had just heard the most terrifying news. Man... this Bella chick must be something else.

"Please tell me you are joking!" he exclaimed.

"I'm not joking, unfortunately for you," Jake said. "She asked me about you and everything!"

"Fuck...goddammit," Aaron cursed.

"Who is Bella Davis?" Macie asked. She looked confused. I don't blame her.

"A total psycho. I can't believe you didn't tell me sooner. I bet this is her handiwork," he said and pointed at the note.

"There is no way you can prove that," Jake shook his head.

"Why don't we just ask her?" I suggested.

"Oh Janey, we can't just march over to her house and ask if she broke our window! She'll totally deny it," Jake said.

True. We have no proof that she did it. But who else could it be? Maybe she was still obsessed with Aaron.

"How about we ask her to hang out with us then sneakily make her tell the truth?" I suggested.

"Yeah, why don't we also tie her up in the basement and torture her until she confesses?" Aaron rolled his eyes.

"Like in the movies! Great idea!" I beamed.

Aaron looked horrified. "I was joking! What the hell Jane," he shook his head in disappointment.

"But no seriously. We should get closer to her. You know what they say, keep your friends close and keep your enemies closer," I said.

Aaron dismissed me. "You do whatever you want but I am not getting any closer to her. She is so annoying, you have no idea."

"Yeah. I don't want her interfering with me and Aaron's relationship," Macie agreed.

These people are no fun, I thought, and sighed. Whoever threw the rock seems serious. What if she tries to do something more dangerous!

The rest of the day was uneventful. I was done hanging out with Jake so I started to walk to my mom's car. I borrowed it so I could come over here. I stopped on my tracks as I spotted Bella watering the flower garden at the front yard. She had her hair up in a ponytail again. Sun shone on her making it look bright and fiery. She was wearing a light yellow sundress that complimented her pale skin. She looks so innocent. Could this be the same girl who was capable of throwing a rock at someone's window?

I know Aaron told me not to approach her but I couldn't help it. Being nosy was one of my weaknesses. I wanted to ask her some questions.

"Hey Bella," I called her quietly so I don't startle her.

She looked up and smiled. "Hey! Jane is it?" she asked.

"Yeap, that's me," I said.

"What can I do for you Jane?" she looked at me curiously.

"Oh, nothing. I was just wondering if I could get to know you a little. Since you are Jake's neighbor and all. Maybe we can be friends?" I smiled. Hoping

38. INTERVIEW WITH A STALKER

she doesn't suspect me.

"Oh! That's very sweet of you. Of course! Why don't you come in and we can talk?" she said brightly

I nodded in agreement and followed her inside.

"Why don't we go to my room and talk?" Bella suggested.

Oh? I get to see Ms. Stalker's room? How exciting.

"That's a wonderful idea," I said.

I was gravely disappointed as soon as I stepped inside her room. It was nothing like how I imagined. It just looked like an ordinary room resided by an ordinary young adult female. Nothing creepy about it. No headless dolls as a decoration or no shrine dedicated to Aaron Morris.

She motioned me to sit down on the chair by the desk.

I immediately went into the interview mode. Time to start grilling this mysterious redhead. "So how long have you known the Morris brothers?" I asked.

"Since middle school!" she chirped.

"Oh? And when did you start to like Aaron?" I asked.

Her eyes turned dark. Too soon?

"Did Jake tell you? What did he tell you?" she looked at me curiously.

"Oh, not much. Just that you had a huge crush on him but he never returned your feelings," I lied. No need to hurt the poor girl's feelings.

She looked down and smiled. "Yeah...I was a bit obsessed with him back then. I still am I guess," she said.

Whaaa....I didn't expect her to admit it so soon.

"You are?" I beamed. Why am I so excited about this?

"Well, I wouldn't say obsessed but I do like him a lot," she confessed. "I think he is an amazing guy. He had this bad reputation in high school but he was never mean to me. And he was just so...handsome. I guess I started to have feelings for him then."

"Oh, I see," I didn't know what to say. She sounds normal so far.

"I guess I went a little overboard with my crush. It became an obsession. I started to do crazy things to get his attention. I even pretended to be his girlfriend to drive away other girls," she sounded sad.

"Whoa...that's crazy!" Jake already told me about all this but I pretended like this was the first time I am hearing about it.

"Yeah. I don't know why I am telling you all this," she giggled.

"I am a good listener," I smiled reassuringly. "You know Aaron liked me but I fell in love with Jake because you can choose who you fall in love with, you know," I said.

"Really?" her eyes turned wide. "Then you know exactly what I am talking about! I couldn't help it. I still can't!"

"So are you like...obsessed with him again?" I pressed.

"No, it's not like that anymore. But I still like him a lot," she said shyly.

Like him enough to throw a rock at his window with a threatening note? I thought.

"So what were you doing around 8 pm last night?" I asked.

"That's an oddly specific question, Jane," Bella laughed.

I hesitated. I asked that question on impulse, she is probably suspicious of me now!

"Erm...I was just wondering because...I think I saw you come out of your house? Sorry, I am being nosy," I laughed nervously.

"I was inside my room the whole time so it couldn't have been me that you saw," she insisted.

I wasn't sure if I believed her but she sounded genuine. If it wasn't her then who was it?

40

39. Running from the Stalker

"I can't believe you went over to her house and asked her questions. You are nuts," Jake remarked when I told him about Bella.

"Tell me something I don't know," I rolled my eyes.

"So what do you think of her? Did she seem like a crazy person?" Jake asked me and looked at me curiously.

"Nope. Not all all. She seemed like a perfectly sane person. Although, she did admit she still likes Aaron," I said.

"Who still likes Aaron?" Aaron walked in. He must've overheard our conversation.

"Bella Davis," I said.

"And how do you know that?" he raised his eyebrows.

"Through her excellent detective skills," Jake replied for me.

Aaron shook his head. "She is just so...ugh," his face was turning red. Wait... is he blushing?

"I can't believe you managed to avoid her this whole time," Jake chuckled.

"I've been very careful," Aaron said.

"She is really not that bad. You should give her a chance. And she is so pretty!" I remarked.

"Hell no. But thanks for the advice," Aaron frowned and left the room.

"Motherfucke-....!!" I heard him screaming outside and it hasn't even been 2 minutes since he left.

Jake jumped out of the couch and ran outside. I followed.

"What happened?" I asked frantically.

"Someone slashed my tire. All four of them," Aaron said. He was red with fury, his fists were closed like he was about to punch someone. "That's it, I'm going to talk to her," he said.

"Bro..." Jake hesitated.

"It couldn't be her! She likes you! Why would she do that to someone she likes? That makes no sense!" I protested.

"Her obsession doesn't make sense! Who else could it be? I'm going over there," he said and stormed over to her house.

Poor Bella. I hope she was ready for Aaron Morris's wrath.

"We should go with him, you know...for safety," I suggested Jake.

"Aaron can handle a girl," Jake said dismissively.

"I meant for Bella. He looks angry," I said. I was seriously worried about her and refused to believe she was the bad guy.

Jake chuckled. "Sure, let's go see what's happening," he said.

"Bella! Open the door, I need to talk to you!" Aaron yelled.

The door flew open almost immediately and Bella stood in front of him wide-eyed.

"Aaron! It's been so long!" she proceeded to hug him but he pushed her away. Oops...denied.

"Save the pleasantries for later. Did you throw a rock at my window and slashed my tire?" Aaron asked. Damn...no hi, how are you?

Her eyes went even bigger. "What are you talking about? I didn't do those things!" She said.

"You didn't write this note?" Aaron took the note out of his pocket and shoved it in her hands.

"No silly. This is not even my handwriting. You should know since I gave you all those letters before," she smiled.

"So what? You could change your handwriting or have someone else write this! It had to be you, Bella. You did crazy shit to me before," Aaron said irritably.

"Yes, I did some things but I owned up to them. I didn't do what you just

39. RUNNING FROM THE STALKER

accused me of so I don't appreciate it. Goodbye," Bella declared and slammed the door shut.

"Well...that settles it," I shrugged.

"I don't believe her," Aaron said gruffly.

Aaaaand we are back to square one.

The next few days everything seemed normal. It was time for us to go on our family trip so Jake and I were hyped up about it. I couldn't believe my parents agreed to let me take him. Nothing ever goes my way so this was exciting.

Jake wrapped his arms around my waist and pulled me onto his lap. His parents were out of town so we had the whole house to ourselves. Well, us and Aaron. But he was seldom home.

We were just about to get it on when we heard a commotion outside. It sounded like someone was arguing outside on the driveway. We could hear it through the open window.

"Now what?" Jake sighed and jumped up then walked to the window, I followed.

I saw Aaron standing outside, practically fuming. Standing in front of him was none other than Bella Davis!

"Oh boy, we better go down there before big bro loses it completely," Jake said and headed outside. Great, more drama.

"I told you a hundred times. I am not going to like you no matter what! Just leave me the fuck alone!" Aaron cried.

"I just don't understand why? Why won't you like me? What's wrong with me?" Bella asked. Sadness enveloped her face.

"What is wrong with you? Are you seriously asking me? You threw a rock at my window, slashed my tire, and now this?" he pointed at his car. It was the first time I noticed the big bold scratch on the side of the car that says, *Let Macie Go.*

Yikes. Aaron loved his car. Whoever did this must not value their life because he'd probably kill him. I hoped Bella was telling the truth and didn't do something like this.

"For the last time! I didn't do this. Why won't you believe me?" Bella looked at Aaron with her big, sad, and pitiful blue eyes. "Sure, I've done some crazy stuff back then but this is low. I would never go this far."

"The hell you won't," Aaron barked. "I've been way too nice but not anymore. You are going to pay for this."

"No I am not," she declared and tried to walk away but Aaron grabbed her wrist.

"Whoa whoa, let's just take it easy," I said to the fuming Aaron. "We don't have proof that it was Bella who did that. It could be anyone!" I announced.

"Who else is obsessed with me and have reasons to hate Macie?" Aaron asked.

"Okay, you got me there," I said and looked at Bella. "You really didn't do this?" I asked.

"NO!" she screamed. "I love Aaron! I would never do anything to hurt him. I want him to love me, that's all I want!"

Oh boy. Maybe she was capable of doing stuff like this. How can she love someone who wouldn't give her the time of his day?

Aaron let go of her. "This isn't over. I will get you back for this," he said.

"Ugh! I didn't do it!" she screamed and ran back to her house.

"GODDAMMIT!" Aaron punched the hood of his car in frustration.

"Let's just calm down, okay? It's not like we can't afford the paint job," Jake remarked.

"It's not about the money. It's about how a psycho girl is trying to come between me and Macie!" Aaron said. "Hey, I need to ask you guys a favor."

"What's that?" I asked.

"Is it cool if me and Macie come to the trip with you guys? I'll drive myself up there and pay for my own hotel room of course. I just need to get away from this craziness for a few days," he said and looked at me with pleading eyes.

I was taken aback by his sudden request but didn't see a problem with him tagging along. I just had to ask my parents if it was okay with them.

"Sure, I'll ask my parents," I smiled.

41

40. Suspect Number Two?

It turned out, my parents had no problem with Aaron tagging along with his girlfriend. More the merrier they said. So off we went, on our family trip. Never in my life have I imagined that I would be vacationing with the Morris brothers. Maybe I was in the twilight zone.

The ride to my grandma's house went smoothly. Except for the fact that Liliana glared at Macy once in a while. I guess she still didn't accept the fact that Aaron would date anyone else except for her.

A thought flashed in my mind. What if it was Liliana who was doing all these crazy things to Aaron?

Nah...no way. She might be a bitch sometimes but she isn't a psycho.

"Stop staring into the distance and pay attention to me," Jake growled in my ear and turned my head to face him.

I came along to their hotel to spend time with him since I wasn't allowed to stay in the hotel with him.

"What are you thinking about? Is it another guy? I'll kick his ass," he said with such a serious expression that it made me giggle.

"Stop being stupid. Who else would I think about?" I said.

Jake shrugged. "I don't know...Carlos?"

"He rejected me then ran away remember?" I laughed.

"Technically, he never did. He ran away because I scared him," Jake said thoughtfully.

"Then I guess I still have a chance with him," I grinned.

Jake stared at me intently. "You are playing with fire here little lady," he raised his eyebrows.

"Pfft...you don't scare me, Morris. If you misbehave I'll go find Carlos. He is cute with his brown eyes and a head full of curls, and...mmfph!" Jake shut me up by smashing his lips against mine and shoving his tongue down my mouth. It is too easy to make him jealous.

He pushed me down the bed and hovered on top of me without breaking the kiss. I was struggling to breathe but his kiss felt so good that I didn't want to stop. I could feel the heat radiating between my legs. I need to make him stop before we go too far.

"Wait...get off of me. We are supposed to go meet up with our parents in a few hours," I said after breaking our heated kiss.

"In a couple of hours but not right now," he leaned down and licked my collarbone.

"Nn...no...Jake! We shouldn't do this right now!" I whined and moaned at the same time.

"Who's gonna stop me?" he growled.

Certainly not me, I thought as I moaned when he slipped his hand inside my bra and fondled my breast.

"I love you Jane," he said and pushed my shirt up some more, then planted kisses on my stomach. My body was burning and I wanted him to make a mess of me.

"Wa...wait...where are Aaron and Macie? What if they come in?" I whimpered.

"They won't. Aaron went out with Macie to some restaurant," he moved down and pulled down my jeans.

"No...Jake!" I cried.

He paused and looked me in the eyes. "Are you saying no? You don't want to?" He gave me his sad puppy eyes that melted my weak heart.

"Ugh fine! You are terrible!" I gave in. It's not like I hated the idea anyway.

He pulled down my underwear and pressed his lips directly on my heated core. I cried out in ecstasy as he licked and thrust his tongue inside me. I hope

40. SUSPECT NUMBER TWO?

they don't hear me moaning in the room next door to us.

He stopped just as I was about to climax. "No...why did you stop?" I whimpered. I was throbbing down there. He smirked and took a condom out then teared up the package with his teeth. I don't know why I found it so sexy because It made me wetter. He positioned himself at my entrance then slammed into me. I gasped loudly and moaned.

"Did you just come? I just put it in," he chuckled.

"That's because you stopped going down on me right before I could, you jerk!" I said in a hoarse whisper.

"Sorry baby, I will make it up to you now," he grinned and kissed me as he slipped in and out of me. I gripped his back and hugged him closer to me so I could hear his racing heart.

41. The Confrontation

Four of us decided to go to an amusement park. It was a nice day out, perfect for some outdoor activities.

"Oh look! A Ferris wheel. Let's ride that, it'll be so romantic," Macie said enthusiastically.

"Booriiing!" Jake and I said at the same time. "We are riding THAT," I said and pointed at a roller coaster that looks like death. Jake nodded in agreement and gave me a high five. Ah...I picked a good one.

"Suit yourselves," Aaron said and smirked. We split up and went to our designated rides.

Few minutes after the ride was over, we went to look for Aaron and Macie but they were nowhere to be found. We walked around for 15 minutes but didn't see them.

"Um...should we be worried?" I asked.

"Nah, they are adults. If they are lost that's not our problem," he shrugged.

I laughed. "Stop being a jerk and call them!" I exclaimed.

"Fine," he grumbled and called Aaron. He put the phone on speaker.

"Jake and Jane! Hurry up and meet me by the Ferris Wheel, NOW!" Aaron screamed over the phone.

Huh? What the hell is going on...

We rushed toward the Ferris Wheel. Aaron was standing near a trash can, breathing heavily. I didn't see Macie anywhere.

41. THE CONFRONTATION

"What happened?" Jake demanded to know.

"Macie is missing," Aaron said.

"Huh? What do you mean?" I asked.

"She said she was going to the bathroom and didn't come back. I asked this lady to check for me but she wasn't in the bathroom! I tried calling too and no answer," he said. His face was twisted into a frown.

"Maybe she got lost and her phone died?" I offered.

"No, that's not it. What should I do?" Aaron looked at us with worry.

"Let's keep looking for her before calling the police or something," Jake said and we all agreed.

We looked for almost twenty minutes. I was about to give up and suggest to call the police then suddenly saw her in the distance. It looked like she was arguing with some guy.

"Aaron! She is over there!" I said and pointed.

Aaron strode over there without wasting any more time. Jake and I followed.

"How could you follow me here, Trevor! You and I are over!" Macie shouted.

Oof...Drama! I'm all ears.

"I never wanted it to be over. I love you!" the guy named Trevor cried.

"What the fuck is going on? Who the fuck are you?" Aaron stepped in and glared at Trevor.

"Macie belongs to me and you took her from me!" Trevor whined.

"Took her? Macie made the decision to be with me. She chose me so take a walk," Aaron snarled.

"How did you find me anyway? We are out of state!" Macie exclaimed.

"I followed you. I've been watching your every move, Macie," Trevor said it like he was proud of himself.

Wait...he followed us all the way here? The dude is a special kind of crazy.

"You've been stalking me!" Macie yelled. I could tell she was freaked out.

An idea clicked in my head when I put the two and two together.

"Um...excuse Mr. Trevor, is it? Were you the one who threw that rock at Aaron's window and slashed his tires?" I asked.

Trevor looked at me intently. "You can't prove shit," he said.

Hold on a minute...

Did Trevor just admit to doing all those things? Well...that was easy.

Aaron moved quickly. He grabbed his collar and lifted him up. "You son of a bitch! You broke my window and slashed my tire? Tell me why I shouldn't kill you right now?

"Because it's illegal?" Trevor offered. Nice going Trevor, you are about to piss the former bad boy even more.

"Guys, please. Stop. You can't fight in the middle of the park. Aaron put Trevor down," Macie interjected.

Aaron glared at him but put him down.

"I am still in love with Macie. We were together for 3 years and then you came out of nowhere and started dating her. She doesn't love you. She loves me, she is just confused," Trevor said.

"That's not true! It's over between us," Macie whined.

"I don't give a fuck how long you dated her or whether she loves me or not. She doesn't want you back so get the fuck out of here before I beat your ass," Aaron barked.

Fear reflected in Trevor's eyes but he didn't back down immediately. He reached into his pocket and pulled out something shiny. It was a switchblade knife. Is he really planning to stab someone over a girl? Jeez.

Jake was silently observing the drama unfold this whole time but as soon as he saw the knife he strode over to Trevor and grabbed his wrist and twisted it until he dropped the knife. He screamed out in pain as Jake held his hand in a painful angle.

"Watch it, you little shithead. I'll break your scrawny little wrist if you don't behave," Jake barked. He looked menacing. I remember being scared of that face but now I find it quite sexy.

"What's going on here?"

We all turned out and saw one of the park's security guards standing in front of us.

"This idiot is harassing my girlfriend," Aaron said.

"That's not true!" Trevor protested.

"Whatever it is, deal with it outside of the park. Or should I call the police?"

41. THE CONFRONTATION

the guard said curtly.

"That's not necessary. I am leaving," Trevor announced and tried to walk away but Aaron grabbed his collar.

"I am not done with you yet. Let's go," he said and dragged him away.

I looked at the guard and smiled reassuringly. "Don't worry. He won't hurt him, we are all friends," I said.

The guard shrugged. "Whatever, I don't get paid enough to deal with this," he said and left.

Jake, Macie, and I followed Aaron outside. He let go of Trevor and glared at him intensely.

"From now on, you stay away from Macie, or I will drag your ass to the cops for harassment. You are lucky I am not charging you for the damages you caused me," Aaron said.

Trevor didn't say anything for a moment.

"Please Trevor, just leave," Macie pleaded.

"Fine, I'll leave. Don't come crying to me if this jerk hurts you," Trevor sighed and walked away.

"Boy...that was pretty dramatic," Jake smirked.

"I am so sorry Aaron. I had no idea Trevor is so hung up on me that he'd follow me here," Macie cried.

"Still...you should've said something when all those weird things were happening," Aaron sounded annoyed.

"I guess you owe Bella an apology, huh?" I remarked. I was glad her innocence was proven.

Aaron looked at me. His eyes were dark as he remembered his confrontation with Bella. "I guess I do," he said.

43

Epilogue

Things went back to normal after the trip. No more Trevor vandalizing Aaron's properties and no more ex-boyfriend drama, at least, for now. Aaron gave Bella an awkward apology which she accepted wholeheartedly. It seems that she decided to ignore Aaron's harsh treatments against her and continued to obsess over him despite him having a girlfriend. What a persistent girl!

It was near graduation so Jake and I prepared for college.

"We are applying at the same college because you are not allowed to be separated from me," he declared.

"Excuse me...don't I have anything to say to this, Mr. Possessive? What if I don't want to go to the same school as you?" I demanded to know.

He leaned closer and stared into my eyes intensely. "You don't?" he asked. His brown eyes were dark and sadness flickered in them.

"Don't look at me like that. That's not fair," I whined.

"What are you talking about? Look at you like what?" he acted obliviously. Jerk.

"Look at me with those sad looking doe eyes to emotionally blackmail me. You think just because you are giving me a cute look I will change my mind about going to a different college," I pouted.

"Well? Did it work? Did I change your mind?" he smirked.

I sighed. "Yes...you evil bastard," I said.

EPILOGUE

He chuckled and kissed me.

"FUCKING HELL!" someone yelled, interrupting us. I jumped out of the bed and almost fell on the floor.

"What the hell, Aaron?" Jake asked irritably.

"It's happening again," Aaron huffed and puffed.

"What's happening?" I looked at him curiously.

"Bella…she is starting it again," he said. He looked genuinely distressed. What's the big deal? I thought.

"I don't get why it's so bad? Can't you just ignore her?" I suggested.

"You tried to ignore Jake, how did that work out for you?" Aaron pointed out.

"HEY! I wasn't stalking her. She liked me from the beginning. Isn't that right Janey?" Jake looked at me lovingly.

"I wouldn't say I liked you from the beginning. You just grew on me," I grinned.

"Guys! Focus! I am having a crisis. I mean, look!" he handed us a booklet.

Jake took the booklet and opened it. I almost snorted as I saw what it was. It was not a booklet, it was a goddamn love letter! At least 10 pages long! I admire her spirit.

"Dude," Jake laughed.

"This isn't funny," Aaron was annoyed.

"You are right. Who writes letters anymore. Especially a one that looks like a research paper. She should've emailed you instead," I said.

"This isn't funny, Jane. She wrote a lot of …weird things. What if Macie sees it and misunderstands me?" Aaron said and looked at us desperately.

"Well then let's go out back and burn it, Jake suggested.

"Wait…no. I don't want that," Aaron said quickly and took it off of Jake's hands.

"Why not?" Jake asked.

"Eh…it took her a lot of effort to write this so I am just gonna keep it," Aaron said quietly.

Awww… Aaron is still being the nice guy to the creepy girl. No wonder she won't give up on him.

"You'll be going back to college next week. Then you can be far away from her and live happily ever after with Macie," I said and smiled reassuringly.

"There's only one problem with that scenario," Aaron sighed. I looked at him questioningly.

"Bella just informed me she is attending my college this semester. So I am screwed," Aaron shook his head frustrated.

True love has no bound I guess.

Three months later...

In the end, Jake got what he wanted. We both got accepted to the same university. He insisted that we move in together. His logic? Some douche might try to hit on me and he might be too far from me to kick his ass. Sigh... what am I going to do with this boy?

But even though he acted tough and possessive he was still the sweet Jake who loved me with all of my quirks. I loved him and he made me laugh with his cringy nicknames and a sick sense of humor. He called me beautiful every day. And when he looked at me with those dark brown eyes full of adoration and lust, I felt like the most beautiful girl in the world. I guess I wasn't the ugly one after all.

The End

Also by Angela Lynn Carver

Stalking Aaron

Aaron Morris had it all. Good looks, a beautiful girlfriend, good grades in college. He only had one problem. He was being stalked by a red-haired nightmare otherwise known as Bella Davis! She was the bane of his existence, a thorn on his side who won't leave him alone no matter what. Will he ever get rid of her or will she continue to annoy him with her unrequited love?

Made in the USA
Columbia, SC
11 March 2021